HOPE ANOTHER WAY

Mary Cantell

Zion Press

Zion Press
1601 Mt. Rushmore Rd, STE 3288
Rapid City, SD 57702

Ordering Information:
Quantity sales. Special discounts are available on quantity purchases by corporations, associations, and others. For details, contact the "Special Sales Department" at the address above.

Hope Another Way/Cantell —1st ed.

ISBN 978-1-63357-321-5

Library of Congress Control Number: 2020936171

First edition: 10 9 8 7 6 5 4 3 2 1

To my beloved husband, all my love, and to the memory of my sweet mother, who nurtured the writing bud in me, thank you. Above all, to my Lord, who guides my mind and heart to write.

The beauty of the world has two edges. . . one of laughter, one of anguish, cutting the heart asunder

—Virginia Woolf

Acknowledgements

It takes a village to write a novel. With each attempt at creating the pages of a fictional world, there's always the true-to-life details that need inserting to render the make-believe plausible. Such as it is with this work. My thanks go to so many who endured my multiple phone calls and inquiries with their patience and kindness:

Adoptions from the Heart
Norristown Fire Department
Plymouth Township Fire Department
Montgomery County Children and Youth Services
Jefferson Hospital
Judy Mobley, first reader
Jay H. Ginsburg, Esq., Adoption Advocates
Ronnie Rotili
My editor, Heather Beck, for her keen eye and kind support of my creative expression.
Rick Bates and the entire editorial team who saw the vision for my manuscript and lent their support in countless ways.
David Welday, thank you for your helpful suggestions and insightful strategies to make my product marketable and outstanding.

Chapter One

Fall 2017
Chester County, Pennsylvania

Misery pressed in like a dull knife. Not enough to pierce a vein or draw blood but enough to scrape the skin raw. Becca leaned on the kitchen table and cradled her head in her hands. A strand of ebony hair drifted out of the loose knot wound at the nape of her neck and fell to the table. She stared at the swirls of wood grain. The continuum of lines and ovals, like an abstract painting, drew her in until her vision blurred. Lost in the moment, she let the water from her eyes drip onto the smooth surface.

Everything had its purpose. Hers? She wasn't sure. Only her heart broke once too often these days. Like an old, beat-up sponge, she sopped up the dirty water of grief and squeezed it out when no one was looking. She was only a bystander in the heated argument between her husband and son and hadn't contributed a word of it. Though it didn't lesson the pain of witnessing the uproar between them. The anger cut through the walls, and their harsh words still echoed in her head. Would they ever get along?

A pair of scissors lay next to a pile of coupons stacked under the glass salt and pepper shakers. The blades glinted in the pool of light cast by the overhead pendant and sent a silent stab to her breast—a long ago memory. Someone must have forgotten to put them away. Hating the clutter, Becca collected the coupons and scissors and marched across the room to the catch-all junk drawer by the sink where she kept miscellaneous things that had collected over the years—old keys, warranties, and dog-eared church tracts she hadn't yet given away. The drawer needed organizing, but she was in no frame of mind to do it now.

Outside the window, the bright yellow swing set she and Paul had purchased for their granddaughter sat in the backyard like a lonely, untended child. She longed to see Tally swinging on it, flying higher and higher the way she liked. The cadence of her voice, her giggles and smiles, all lent a pleasant demeanor to the home. A deafening quiet rose in her absence. Without the child around, the palpable hush rendered the house a tomb. She pulled the cord and let the blinds down.

As she stepped away from the window, an odd, acrid scent seeped into the room. Evening barbecues were not uncommon in the small Chester County town, or maybe the next-door neighbors were burning leaves. She inhaled again. She loved the bourbon-like scent of kindling leaves, but this was different. Something wasn't right. Piqued by the burnt smell, she turned for the hallway and saw what she didn't expect. Her breath caught.

"Oh, no!" she shrieked. Smoke puffed from under the door to the converted basement where her son and daughter-in-law temporarily stayed when they weren't incarcerated for one reason or another. At first, Paul was against it, insisting they take up their living responsibilities elsewhere without their assistance, but at Becca's resolve, he acquiesced. At least she could keep an eye on them if they lived under one roof. She raised her fist and pounded on the door. "Jason? Lark? Are you down there?" An image of them lying unconscious from smoke inhalation flashed in her mind. Her pulse ticked faster. Then her thoughts turned to Tally, who was at her great-grandmother's house visiting for the weekend. Thankfully, the child was safe. Becca pressed the tip of her finger to the doorknob. Warm but not hot. She pulled open the door. An onslaught of smoke smacked her face.

"Jason...Lark!" No reply. She sucked in a deep breath and took a hesitant step forward while pulling her T-shirt over her nose. She braced herself for what came next.

Becca raced down the steps, blinded by the heavy smoke, and felt her way around the room with her arms extended as she desperately searched for Jason and Lark.

"Anybody here?" she managed to choke out while stumbling into the furniture. She poked and pressed her hands into the cushions of the fold-out couch and the side chair. "Kids...are you down here?" Silence. She ran back up the stairs trying hard not to breathe.

"Paul," she cried, her voice breaking. She gasped for breath.

Her husband rushed into the kitchen, his face etched with alarm.

She held her throat and coughed out, "Fire—basement."

"Good Lord, have mercy." He pushed past her and hastened down the hall toward the basement door.

"No, Paul," she pleaded. Her voice pitched with fervor. "Don't go down"—she shook her head—"No one's there. I checked." She winced at the thought of him barging into the smoky inferno and yanked on his sleeve to pull him away."

His face folded. "They must have left."

"Already?" Her heart sunk.

"Probably sometime after the fight," he said and raced toward the kitchen.

The emotional turmoil between her husband and son had broken her spirit, but for Jason to leave so abruptly instead of sleeping on it, this caused Becca's heart to bleed all over again. A mental glimpse of Jason striking a match popped into her head. *Retaliation?* No, he couldn't have been responsible. That wasn't like Jason. Or Lark. Neither of them even smoked as far as Becca knew. They may have been delinquents, but why would they intentionally burn down the house where they lived rent free... where their own child lived? It didn't add up.

"Get out, *now*," Paul commanded. He came back down the hall with a wet towel and packed it tightly along the space under the door. Then he took her by the shoulders and aimed her toward the back door of the kitchen. "We need to get out right now."

She froze. "But the dog...where's Toby?"

"Don't worry, I'll find him," he shouted as he reached for the phone. "Right now, I'm calling the fire department."

Chapter Two

Becca dashed out of the house. She scurried to the bottom of the driveway and turned around at the curb to face the house. Wearing only a thin cotton T-shirt, goose flesh prickled her bare arms. She shivered partly from the plummeting temperature but mostly from pure nerves. The Indian summer day had been a balmy seventy-eight degrees a few hours ago. Presently, it felt at least ten degrees cooler. Adrenaline coursed through her body, and her legs wobbled like two sticks of jelly.

The last remains of sunlight flickered in the tall, dark pines on the hill behind the house. Like sentries, the trees stood stalwart and composed, their arms raised to heaven as though praying. Normally, she loved this time of day when sunlight bronzed the landscape with brilliant copper light in a final bow to nightfall. Though now, the finale staged before her tainted all past appreciation. The lusterless light at the horizon hung like a tarnished coin through the rising din of smoke. A fire alarm rose in the distance.

Becca's heart weighted heavy as a wrecking ball in her chest. Memories flew back to the day she and Paul first bought the Cape Cod. Their first home.

"*It's perfect,*" she gushed. They both loved the suburban aesthetic; the quaintness of the tree-draped hills and valleys soothed her soul, unlike the big city with its amalgam of dirt and noise. Like a Wyeth painting come-to-life.

Her eyes darted around the neighborhood. Every home on the block maintained a well-tended charm; though this house she shared with Paul, as it sat among the jewels of the neighborhood, presented itself more like a *before* picture. As much as she and Paul tried to keep things spruced up, their house sat like a disheveled dog one step away from a good shampoo and a pair of clippers. A broken shutter needed replacement, and the once eggshell-colored siding had darkened under the mold on the north-facing side. The chipped white fence could use another coat, and as far as the barberry bushes, they had a mind of their own and snagged her skin every time she contended with the thorny branches. She was not a gardener, and Paul, a high school science teacher, was not a handyman.

Smoke rose and curled around the side of the house and up toward the frame. Flames licked and lapped, sending charred bits into the air. The fire desperately consumed the clapboard as though it held a vendetta. Their home on Scarlett Oak Lane, once their pride, was now disintegrating into a pile of embers. Tears burned in her eyes.

Becca offered a quick, panic-stricken prayer for God's miraculous intervention. They couldn't lose the house. *Where was Paul?* Her heart raced. Moments later, he hastened around from the side yard with Toby in his arms just as a bulky red firetruck squeezed up the driveway.

"This way," Paul shouted as he rotated one arm like a windmill, signaling the direction. "Here, over here." The firemen pulled a thick black hose across the lawn while Paul ran ahead of them like a border collie herding sheep.

A few of the neighbors across the street stared from their driveways like frightened meerkats. Jane, her next-door neighbor, peeked her head out the door. Soon, she came rushing over and put an all-too-sympathetic arm around Becca's shoulder.

"Everything's gonna be okay, honey," Jane encouraged with a squeeze. "Not to worry, the firemen'll put it out."

Through her tears, Becca half-nodded, but Jane's syrupy-sweet drawl couldn't tamp down the anxiety swirling in her bowels. Becca's stomach spun as though it were a wash cycle at top speed. *Will the fire spread? Would they have a place to sleep tonight?* She struggled to control her tortured thoughts while Jane reassured her things would be all right.

Chapter Three

Four weeks later

The apartment Becca and Paul now called home—the only suitable place they could find on short notice after fire destroyed much of their house—was more akin to a doll's house. Most of the furniture from their old residence didn't fit inside the scaled-down floor plan and needed to be stored. Becca made all of the arrangements. She doubted an outdoor storage unit was the best place for her things—even short term. But this was her only choice. She cringed at the image of mold and mildew inhabiting their belongings as she handed the manager of U-Store-It a check for the first month's storage fee.

"Everything all right?" Becca asked Paul, who sat at the kitchen table wedged inside the tiny breakfast nook. His jaw set like flint, and his receding hairline—more salt than pepper—along with the halogen-bright overhead lights, which illuminated every forehead line, aged him a decade. Becca remembered the time they first met at a friend's outdoor party. His hair was as rich and black as the charcoal briquets in the barbeque pit before the chef lit the match.

"Yep," he replied. "Everything's fine." His tone belied the words, and he exhaled a forced huff. "I'm just doing what I should have done before." His potent stare at the pile of credit cards laid out on top of the bare oak table, along with the scissors he held like a dagger, resembled a wild animal about to pounce on its prey. "It's time we learn to stop depending on these things." He picked up one of the cards and shoved the blades down the middle. *Snap.*

Becca flinched. His decisiveness surprised her. Although Paul had a soft, sweet side, when push came to shove, he didn't fall down. She pulled out a chair and sat down across from him. He picked up another card. The crisp sound of the hard plastic as he cut it into pieces confirmed his resoluteness. *Snap, snap, snap.*

"Don't worry, I'm not cutting up all of them." The corners of his mouth lifted as though to console her. "I know what I'm doing."

She wasn't convinced, but she had more on her mind than their credit. "Are you sure we're doing the right thing?"

"Right?" he barked. "These things will have us hamstrung for the next ten years. I know we'll need credit at some point with everything going on, but I don't want an albatross around our necks later when we're retired and—"

"No, I mean about Jason and Lark. Kicking them out last month. I still don't know how we could have done that."

"They'll be fine." Paul put the scissors down and folded his hands together. "Besides, they weren't *kicked* out, Becca." He spoke measuredly, as though explaining a child's lesson. She wished he didn't think of her as one of his science class students. "It was Jason's choice to break the rules. Actions have consequences. It wasn't an arbitrary or hard-nosed decision. We've been over this before."

"But he's just a boy," she protested.

"A boy?" His voice rose. "Becca, he's almost twenty-three"—he threw his hand up— "and a father, for Pete's sake. How's the boy—the *man*—going to grow up if we keep taking care of him? He can't even take care of himself, let alone his family." He shook his head. "Thank God we have custody of Tally. Lord knows how she'd end up otherwise."

"It's only *partial* custody," Becca insisted.

"Better this than having none."

"I know." She sighed. "But we don't even know where Jason and Lark are living now." She hung her head in her hands.

"Let them live with *her* parents." His voice pitched. "There's no room here—barely enough for us now. And we didn't exactly live in the Taj Mahal before, so..."

Becca hated the confrontation. The harsh words scraped and poked unnecessary holes into her sensibilities. "Poor girl has no parents, remember? You know, there's just Athena."

"That's what I meant." Paul pushed away from the table and paced the length of the narrow galley kitchen in silence until he erupted again like an unsettled volcano. "He took the car out without permission and then scraped the side door up." Paul underscored each indiscretion with a pronounced nod. "No respect for me, or you, for that matter. No sense of responsibility. He'll probably get locked up again with the path he's on."

Becca couldn't bear seeing her son imprisoned again, or worse, bailing him out. They already bore enough financial debt as it was.

"No job. No accountability. He'll probably start dealing again, right? Or worse. I mean he's ripe for it, and then—"

"Okay, okay." She held her hands up in mock defeat. His incessant litany of Jason's delinquency, like the whine of a rusty wheel, irked her. "But he's *out* of jail now, so let's hope for the best."

"But now, *she'll* be going back, probably. That's how it's always been," he mused. "In and out."

Embarrassed by the truth, Becca dropped her head again. Her heart bled at her granddaughter's plight. Wayward parents, the ferrying back and forth between their home and Lark's grandmother's. She bristled inside and wished the child could remain with her and Paul full-time instead of serving as a shuttlecock in a badminton game.

"It's just not fair," Becca whined.

"Life isn't fair, Bec. It's just the cards we've been dealt."

She shook her head. "It's my fault. Everything that's happened with Jason...from before."

Her ex-husband's face flashed in her mind. The memory of their life together haunted her once more. Now, it reared again—the unanswered question she mulled over for so long: How badly did her horrific first marriage mess Jason up? She questioned herself—and God—so many times.

"What?" Paul sat down. "What are you talking about?" He reached across the table and took her hand.

"If I hadn't left Rob and taken Jason away, maybe things would be different now. He'd be more responsible, maybe? Or not be doing drugs. He'd have turned out...I don't know, tougher?"

Her ex-husband's image snaked through her head. Short-fused. Reckless. She saw it in Jason—the same irresponsible nature she saw in her first husband. An inherited trait? She liked the strong and silent types, but Rob had a wild streak and chased her so long that submission was inevitable. He'd murmured, Your God is *my* God into her ear, until one day, his words waxed straight into her heart. She shivered now at how gullible she had been all those years ago.

"Bec, you can't take responsibility for someone else's choices. He makes his own decisions, plays by his own rules. How many parents have done the good and proper thing by their kids and they *still* go astray?" He gently squeezed her hand. "Remember the Ormonds? They practically held a yardstick to those kids... held them to the letter, and they still messed up."

Despite the tragedy of the Ormond children, her own situation overshadowed it. The angry words between Paul and Jason the last time they were together echoed in her head. Time had dulled the volume, but the fallout from their choice words still rang clearly. She'd hoped and prayed the situation would settle into a fine dust and be swept away, but it would take a while before things would be right between any of them.

Was Jason—with no blood shared with Paul—easier to dismiss than his own flesh and blood would have been? Stepson versus biological. Was there a difference? Though she understood how much Paul had been stretched to the breaking point. Anyone would have reacted the same. He had done so much for Jason through the years—even as much as adopting him.

Paul let go of her hand and went to the sink. He took a glass from the drainboard and filled it with tap water.

"You want some water?" he asked.

She made a face. "Not *that* water. Don't we have any filtered water?"

He downed the glass and refilled. "This is good enough for me." He chugged another gulp. "Shuffling in and out," he continued while motioning back and forth with his hand. "Never contributing. We've been used, Becca." His tone softened. "Can't you see that?" He quirked an eyebrow.

"I know, Paul, but it's what parents do...they—"

"Let their children walk all over them? By the way, are they even together anymore?" He opened the refrigerator door, pulled out a bottled water, and set it on the table in front of her.

"Jason and Lark?" she blurted. "I hope so."

"I mean, exclusively."

The question hung heavy.

"Why?" The clash between reality and her hopes surfaced again. Now, her son was possibly a loser in love, too.

He shrugged. "Just a hunch. Drugs are like a mistress, of sorts."

"They love each other," she snapped. "I'm sure of it."

Becca recalled Jason's over-the-moon face when he first told her and Paul about his new girlfriend. She'd never seen him so excited about anything or anyone before, except for the gift of tickets to see the Philadelphia Phillies play in the all-stars game at the Vet when he was six. Always impulsive as though time were chasing him, Jason made his decision on the fly to ask Lark for her hand in marriage after knowing her for only a few months, and it concerned Becca when they got married so quickly. Her exotic looks were most likely the draw as she resembled the model Iman.

"Maybe he'll find a job. A real one this time." Hurt by another rip into her son's life, she tried to paint her own version outside the lines of reality, if only to convince herself. "And he'll be able to take care of them like he should. It's been so hard because of the bad economy."

Paul gave a snort. "You're going to blame the economy for everything? How about his flagrant sense of entitlement?"

Becca couldn't think of a good defense and knew he was right. There was a time when she thought helping Jason and Lark would be a step toward improving their children's lives. Now, their efforts lent more to enabling.

"If it weren't for us and the grandmother..."

"Athena," Becca offered with a sigh.

Even though Lark's grandmother shared unofficial custody of Tally, she was not, in Becca's opinion, fit to be a guardian, not even part-time. She and Paul were. They had everything Tally needed and could give her the moon and stars. A familiar ache rose inside her chest. The pain for her son and daughter-in-law chafed, but her heart completely tore when it came to the little girl. The sparkle in Paul's eye when the child climbed onto her husband's lap was unmistakable. Becca's heart melted at the sight of them so close and begged of God: What's delaying our adoption request, Lord? Why is this taking so long? The questions burned within her.

Chapter Four

"Hello."

"Hello, there," came the cheerful voice. "Pastor Benson here."

"Oh, hi, Pastor." Becca's mood lifted at the sound of his soothing, fatherly voice.

"Hope all is well there." A man of the cloth, Pastor Benson always maintained an upbeat attitude. "Just wanted to confirm our appointment Friday? Two o'clock still good?"

"Yep, I'll be there."

"Okay, then, my dear. See you then."

****

Grace Fellowship Church stood like a beacon on the hill overlooking the small town of Phoenixville. The pastor's late-model gray Audi sat under a large oak tree. His secretary Margie's bright orange Volkswagen sat beside it. Becca pulled in and parked opposite the cars. Desperation over her circumstances hung like a white surrender flag she hoped he could tear down for her, or maybe this was just some kind of cruel lesson from God she would be forced to battle on her own.

The sweet folks at Grace once laid out the welcome mat for her and Paul the first time they attended the morning service eleven years ago. Bonds formed quickly between Becca and a few of the ladies, who treated her practically like royalty; though, now, doubts crept about what people really thought of her and Paul since the fire. They'd lost the house. Sporadic attendance. Wayward son and daughter-in-law. The dregs of the church, but, at least, they weren't pitifully always looking for handouts, Now, they had another issue on their plates, regarding custody of Tally. It appeared the County wouldn't validate their custodial rights to their own granddaughter. She wondered what kind of joke God was playing. If not God, someone else was orchestrating their bad luck.

Pastor Benson's office sat on the lower level of the church, currently under construction. The renovation project was a long time coming and on the church's prayer list for over a year. With the accrued building funds, they were finally able to contract the work and update the wing housing the Sunday school rooms and also repair the sink holes in the parking lot.

Through the narrow cutout, she made her way down the dusty hallway, sheathed in plastic, toward his office. In a separate area just outside, her good friend, Margie Palmer, glanced up from her computer.

"Hey, there," Margie said, brightly. Wearing an ear-to-ear grin, the stocky brunette rose and circled around the desk. She held both arms out as though about to take flight. "So good to see you, woman." She wrapped her arms around Becca in a warm, sisterly hug.

"Same here, Margie." At ease in her presence—one of the few women at the church she bonded with early on—Becca effortlessly returned the hug and the smile.

"It's been awhile." Margie went back around her desk and sat down. "Have a seat." She gestured toward the brown plaid loveseat across from her desk. "Pastor's on a call. He should be wrapping up soon."

The squeal of drilling erupted through the walls.

"Could the neighborhood get any busier?" Becca said, wryly. "There's construction projects everywhere. Like the whole town has gone development rogue."

"Tell me about it. I could barely get into the parking lot this morning," Margie said. "Half the street is closed off because of that shopping center construction project."

Becca eyed the stacks of wicker baskets piled up on the floor next to Margie's desk.

"What are all the baskets for?"

"Oh, it's for the Welcome Wagon outreach ministry—mainly for families new to the area, especially ones with kids. Just some things they might need." Margie bent over and poked through the contents. "Post-it notes, candles, little tool kits." She held up a package of colored markers and then tossed it back into the pile. "Hey, so how's everybody doing? I haven't seen any of you all in a while." She paused. "Oh, and the fire"—she sympathetically shook her head— "I'm so sorry, Becca." Margie's brown eyes softened. "We took up a collection the minute we heard."

Becca inwardly recoiled at the image of her beloved Cape Cod as it went up in smoke. "Oh, we're okay." She nodded as convincingly as she could. "Thanks, so much for the love gift. So generous of everyone, really."

"How did it start?" Margie cocked her head. "Did they identify the source?"

The nightmare-turned-reality of seeing her house char and crumble as she helplessly watched branded the surreal image forever in Becca's mind. Despite not wanting to relive that desperate hour, the memory came rushing back—the blast of adrenaline that had coursed through her body, the sinister smoke curling up into the sky, and the blaring sound of the alarm. Her body tensed with the remembrance.

"I vaguely remember one of the firemen pointing to the basement window after they got the fire out. He said it probably started there, but he wasn't definite about it," she explained with a shrug. "He didn't call it arson but couldn't rule it out either."

Margie slowly shook her head. "I'm so sorry."

"We've put it behind us—you know, as much as we can."

She nodded. "It's all you can do, I guess." She paused. "And Jason...how's he doing?"

Becca braced and swallowed hard. "Oh." She hesitated to dig too deeply into the dirty laundry of her life, even though Margie was someone she trusted. "Well, he's Jason. What can I say?" She raised her hands in an *oh, well* gesture.

"Is he still in—" Margie hesitated.

"Prison?" Becca finished her sentence. "Actually, no, he's paroled." She gave a reticent smile. "At least, for now. And we're blessed to have Tally, thankfully. We wouldn't want it any other way."

"Terrific news," Margie exclaimed, clapping her hands in the manner of a giddy schoolgirl. "He's a great kid."

Becca nodded, grateful someone else saw the good in her son. He'd traveled a rocky path for so long. She held out hope that in spite of his bad choices, his life would turn around one day.

"I know, but he's got some things to work out."

"Yeah, I'm sure. We all do," Margie mused. "I'm glad he's out now. Tell him to come by the church. I'd love to see him."

"Let's just hope he stays out," Becca replied.

A sliver of doubt crept in. She thought about the fight between her son and Paul, and just where he and Lark were living now, God only knew.

"Oh, think positive, Becca," she replied. "He's married now, right?"

Becca nodded.

"Oh." Margie raised her index finger. "Sounds like Pastor is just finishing up," she whispered. "Paper walls."

Becca was glad their time was running short; discussing her son's life any further would be painful. What Margie didn't know wouldn't hurt her. She'd been his Sunday School teacher, and there was always a mutual fondness between them. How embarrassing to admit he'd become a delinquent. The stigma it bore on her was something she wished for no mother to endure. The weight of her concern had caused her to start smoking again, something she swore she'd never do.

Pastor Benson's door opened, and he peeked his head around the side.

"Becca, come on in." He motioned with his hand. "Sorry to have kept you waiting."

Thin walls being what they were, she hoped none of the private things she planned to share with the pastor leaked out and that Margie wouldn't be tempted to eavesdrop.

Chapter Five

"It's crazy," Becca said, raising her voice. "I just don't understand why the foster kinship program hasn't moved into full adoption status. The County's policy on this is stated plainly in the letter they sent us when we started taking care of Tally in January over two years ago. We're in our third year now"—she raised three fingers—"I'd love to know what's going on with these people. We've waited long enough."

"I see," Pastor Benson said. "A lot going on here." He leaned forward in his high-back leather chair. The plaques and pictures on the walls behind him vouched for his advanced education and degrees in pastoral counseling as well as the ministry. The seventy-five-year-old man was as sharp as they came and didn't look anything even close to his chronological age. "So, basically, you wish to adopt little Tally?" His question came as more of a statement. "You and Paul?"

"Yes, Pastor, we adore her and believe we can offer so much more than..." She pursed her lips. "Well, at least, better than her parents. In and out of jail...it's so hard to stand by and witness their situation. If they want to throw their lives away...well, I'll be—let's just say I refuse to sit by and let it happen, but we feel it's so hopeless."

"I'm sure it's heartbreaking." His pale blue eyes softened in the folds of his face and reminded her of a Chinese shar-pei puppy. "So, what did the County say? Have you gone through the vetting process and—"

"Children and Youth? Oh, yes, of course. We've been questioned, vetted, and interviewed—everything short of a lie detector test and a blood sample. The foster kinship program is fine, but having to share Tally with Athena, the other grandmother—actually, it's Tally's *great*-grandmother—you remember her story, right?" She shook her head. "Terrible arrangement."

"How does Tally feel about it?"

"About us and the adoption—or?"

"The other woman, Athena. Does Tally enjoy spending time with her?"

Becca envisioned Tally's face—the way her nose pressed up against the window when she was ready to be picked up from a weekend at Athena's, the way she scampered out of the house and down the weedy sidewalk with her suitcase flapping at her side.

"She's never told me one way or the other how she feels about Athena, but by the looks of things, I'd say she could take her or leave her."

"I see," he said, rubbing his chin with the back of his hand.

"And Athena's house is in the sketchy part of town on the north side of the county. I hate going there. My stomach is tied up in knots all the way. Worried sick I'll get hit by a stray bullet or carjacked," she lamented. "It breaks my heart to see the neighborhood degenerate to such a sad state... graffiti-covered walls and trash-strewn sidewalks."

Pastor Benson pursed his lips.

"So, to answer your question, I'm not sure, Pastor. There's been nothing verbally expressed, but I'd say that Tally was anxious to get away from there."

"I can understand your concern," he said, shifting in his chair.

"I mean I don't want to label the woman unfit, but some of the things she says, I have to say...well, it sometimes makes my skin crawl. I don't believe her home is a healthy environment for Tally. I wouldn't leave my dog alone with her."

Pastor Benson's features knit as he patiently listened to Becca explain the gritty details of her situation: The story of her son and daughter-in-law's financial difficulties, how they'd been staying with her and Paul until the fight, and how Becca always held out hope for a more amicable relationship between her kids and the law, especially because of Tally.

"And your new place—the apartment? How are you and Paul doing?"

"We're all okay. Paul's back at work, and the new apartment is fine. It's a little cramped, but we've been managing." She glanced over to the window. "It's less than a mile from here on Parkside Avenue, adjacent to the park." She brightened. "For Tally, it's been great. She already has a new friend—our neighbor down the hall, Miss Bea, a sweet older lady. And she has a little garden to tend, courtesy of Miss Bea. Tally is crazy over the chance to grow her own flowers."

Pastor's lips curled up. "Well, sounds like things are not all bad for you."

Becca smiled inwardly, thinking of Miss Bea and how she came over to welcome them the day after they'd moved in, and, later, asking Tally if she'd like to help with a plot of ground out back next to her patio.

"I guess not all is bad, but..." She bit off the rest of what she wanted to say.

"Thank God for small favors, right?" He smiled. "Tell you what," he began and slapped his palm on the desktop. "I have some thoughts. I'd like to mull them over a bit." He leaned back and rested his elbows on the arms of his chair as he steepled his fingers. "I'm not sure how this whole adoption thing will work out, but I'm going to pray about it, and I suggest you and Paul do, too. Also, I'd advise you to get a lawyer."

"But, Pastor, I *do* pray."

He held his palm up. His wedding ring appeared smooth and thin from wear. "Listen, Becca, I know you do. Certainly, I know. But please just give it some more time." He pointed his index finger to the ceiling. "And *he* knows, too." He paused. "All things work together...," he added.

Becca knew the rest of the verse. She had quoted the words many times for the benefit of not only herself but mainly for others. It was easy to recite it then. Their problems weren't hers. She bore no emotional investment other than pure sympathy and concern. Hearing the verse now, however, the words sounded hollow. She stared out the window.

"Becca, is there something else bothering you?" His brow furrowed. "I mean, besides Tally and the slow walk by the County?"

She drew back to him and then lowered her gaze, hesitant to respond. It would be easier to keep the hurt inside, and she would rather delete the question if she could. The stillness in the room hung precipitously, and she could feel the weight of his words... his peering eyes. Could he see her soul? Or the spiritual calluses that grew from lack of faith?

"I understand you've gone through a lot with the fire, the move, and the new apartment and everything." He folded his hands together. Moments later, he opened his Bible. Reading aloud, his words fell all around her but somehow didn't reach into her soul. The chasm was too deep. She believed the scripture, but no sooner did the verse leave the pastor's lips the words evaporated.

Pain pierced her eyes. Tears hovered at the brim, and she swiped them away, hoping he didn't notice. She winced at her stubby fingernails, embarrassed they weren't long and polished as she had once kept them. Chewed up from worry, they resembled a child's. Why bother polishing bitten-down nails? Even tackier.

His soft eyes crinkled as he gave her a sympathetic look. There was no way she could continue keeping her thoughts captive any longer. "I'm not sure how I..."

"I'm listening," he said, his voice just above a whisper.

"It's Jason."

"Jason? Is he in some kind of trouble?"

Everyone in the church knew of Jason's incarceration history; it was no secret.

"Pastor, I'm not totally certain, but I think he deliberately started the fire. Or Lark."

Finally, the words were out. The pressure lifted. While she held mixed feelings, deep down she knew it was right to let go of the pressing thoughts that weighed on her heart.

Pastor Benson's countenance crumpled. "Jason? Oh, my word, no."

"He and Paul had an argument. It was rough. I mean, I don't want to believe my son would go that far to get revenge, but I go back and forth wondering."

Becca shared the details of the night the fire started in the basement. Still, she wanted to preserve her son's reputation by implicating his wife could be equally responsible, if not solely. It hurt to put the blame on him, but what choice did she have?

"Perhaps it was an accident? A burning cigarette?" A firm line drew to his mouth.

Becca shook her head. "Believe me, at first, I thought that just maybe it was a cigarette. But I don't think so."

"How's that?"

"Because he doesn't smoke." Becca folded her arms across her chest. "Lark doesn't either. Neither he nor Lark. I've never seen an ashtray in their room—ever."

Pastor pressed his lips together. "Doesn't sound like the Jason I know." He fingered the smooth gold edges of his black leather-bound King James Bible. "I can't imagine that boy—young man," he said, correcting himself, "doing something so egregious."

"I don't want to believe it. Really, I don't. I've never brought it up with anyone—not even Paul. But maybe something in him just snapped." She bit the inside of her lip. "I just have this sinking feeling... just have to wonder is all."

Becca cast her gaze out the window. The clear afternoon sun shone brightly, and through the muted sounds of drilling, everything seemed right with the world. All except her own personal place in it. Her mind went back to the night of the fire, and she wondered if it wasn't her son who'd set the fire, then who did?

Chapter Six

Spring 2018

"Hey, what do you say we walk to church today?" Becca stood at the kitchen window and peeked out. "Looks nice outside." She yanked the cord of the blinds and lifted the sash. The morning held a nip of dampness from the overnight rain, and the freshly cleansed air lent an aroma of warm honey. She took a deep breath. "Smells nice, too."

"Mom-Mom? Why don't I just live with you and Pop-Pop?"

Becca stopped short, taken aback at the child's out-of-the-blue candor. "But you do live with us, baby."

"No, I mean *just* here—not at Mom-Mom Athena's."

"So, you don't like being at Athena's house?"

"Not, really."

Becca knelt down to meet her gaze at the table. "You never told us, Tally. How long has this been going on?"

The child shrugged.

"Pop-Pop and I want you to be with us, too, baby." She patted Tally's arm. "We're working very hard on making it happen." Her heart stirred.

Becca and Paul had waited so long to get things moving with the adoption process that the wheels of progress had all but ground to a halt.

"Is Pop-Pop coming to church with us today?"

The sweetness in her granddaughter's voice never failed to soften her heart. "Yes, baby, Pop-Pop's coming."

Tally beamed. Her eyes, big as chocolate brown saucers, brightened. "Oh, that's *perfect*." She placed her Fingerling mini doll inside the brand-new little purse Becca found at the local thrift store. Tally had asked for one even before her fifth birthday while they were shopping together, and Becca tittered at the idea. Her granddaughter obviously wished to emulate her—the highest form of flattery.

Becca smiled inside. *Yes, it is perfect.*

Paul popped his head around the corner of the kitchen. "Did I hear my name in here?" he asked in a tone of feigned innocence.

"Pop-Pop!" Tally jumped up from the table.

He bent down and lifted her up into his arms.

"Now, Pop-Pop," she began. "You need to behave in church today."

"I do?" he asked and broke into a smile that grew into a chuckle at the child's serious demeanor.

"Yes, Pop-Pop," Becca said with a wink. "No talking—and no cell phone."

Mock chagrin drew into Paul's face as he turned the corners of his lips downward and bowed his head.

"Yes, I'll try to remember not to disrupt the service today." He patted his Oxford blue shirt pocket where he kept his cell. "I promise, I won't even touch it." He put her down and reached for the keys from under the kitchen spice cabinet and raised his right hand as a sign of confirmation.

"And the same for you, I might add, right?" Becca looked at Tally. Without waiting for an answer, she placed both hands on Tally's shoulders and guided her out of the kitchen. "Now, please go clean you face and brush your teeth. I bought you a new toothbrush."

"The princess one?"

"The princess one," Becca answered. "Now, go."

****

Becca held Tally's hand and Paul took her other as they made their way as a trio along Parkside Avenue. The quiet, tree-lined street was lined with Victorians and Tudors and only a few blocks away from Grace Fellowship. On their way to church together as a family, Becca's heart sparked with joy. She soaked in the moment. It didn't get much better than this.

On the approach to the final block before reaching the church, the sounds of a construction project came from the far end of a strip mall. In the near distance, workers at the sight were busy erecting another store.

"So much construction around here." Becca adjusted her sunglasses. "It's everywhere, lately."

"Progress," Paul replied.

"Construction on a *weekend*? Is nothing sacred these days?" One of the workers guffawed and another stood guzzling down a can of Red Bull as they passed.

"Must be a deadline job. They'll be making a nice amount of cash for it, too."

As the morning sun peeked through the budding trees, Becca's gut cinched. Her blood turned icy. She dropped Tally's hand. Her nerves tightened as she studied the taller of the two men. He wore a white painter's cap with a beige work shirt loosely tucked inside the waistband of hunter green pants. He ambled toward a pile of lumber as her heart did double time. The man bore an uncanny resemblance to her ex-husband. *Could it be?*

"Hold my hand, Mom-Mom," Tally said, breaking the moment.

"Oh," Becca replied, rattled by the incongruity of it all. She struggled to keep her wits and dropped her hand back into Tally's tiny fingers. She gave a gentle squeeze. "Sorry, baby."

In all the time they were together, she could count the number of times her ex had attended the old Baptist chapel after they were married. So, it made sense, if it were him, that he was working on a Sunday and not in church on the Lord's day. Becca recalled the few times he'd put on his best sport coat and pleated dress pants and painfully made his way into the church at Christmas and again at Easter. Twice a year. He thought he was doing her a favor. God only knew what went through his head as he sat stiff-backed against the wooden pew and held the hymnal with his rough, nicotine-stained fingers. That was about it for his spiritual worship. He stopped keeping in touch with her and Jason long ago. Though, sporadically, he remembered to send his son a card for his birthday but ended the practice after Jason turned eighteen. So be it, she thought. He'd tried.

Becca's insides tightened as images popped in her head of their past—the beatings, the knife. Although he had apologized profusely afterward, his words couldn't break through the wall of protection she'd erected. Out of fear, she fled emotionally and swore she wouldn't subject her son to that kind of atmosphere. When she'd first become infatuated with him, he could do no wrong. After a while, his dark side emerged, and the time he once frightened her to death, she saw a shadow looming over her paradise. The relationship thereafter remained on the trash heap of history. Buoyed by a resolve she didn't know she had, and after only one counseling session, she packed her bags, picked up her son from school and was gone.

Becca let go of Tally's hand again and rummaged inside her purse for something—anything—to quell her sudden queasiness. She reached down into the crevice where things sometimes nestled, like the barrette she thought she'd lost, and another time, to her surprise, a neatly folded ten-dollar bill. Nothing but a few coins lay at the bottom today, along with her wallet, cellphone, lipstick, nail kit, and the gold pen Paul had given her.

Paul put his hand to the small of her back. "You okay, Bec?"

With a nod, she forced a half-smile to assuage him and hoped he wouldn't probe further. She didn't want to bring up her ex, or his look-alike, especially not on a Sunday.

"Oh, look," she said with feigned lightness, "there's the church already. It didn't take us long at all."

As they turned the corner, Becca glanced back at the construction site. A trickle of perspiration gathered under her arms as a knife image swirled in her head. She told herself he wasn't going to ever hurt her again and fought the painful memory. The reason? This man was an illusion. Her former husband was dead.

Chapter Seven

The word Becca had received years ago was that her first husband had fallen while mountain hiking. He tumbled down the steepest part of the ridge and landed in the ravine two hundred feet below. A freak accident no one could have survived. She wouldn't attend the funeral of the man who made her life into a bad dream and didn't bother asking when or where it was. The mountaintop where he fell was far away, and she lost track of his side of the family—what was left of them—years before. The whole thing was bittersweet. The bitter part was her memory of him, forever stained. The sweet was that she no longer had to live her life as though tiptoeing on a tightrope without a safety net, and he would no longer be able to hurt her or Jason anymore.

Becca studied the man. Dirty blonde streaks poked out from under his painter's cap; her ex's had been dark brown. She breathed a sigh. A lightness filled her until she became almost giddy. She'd been here before, thinking she saw a familiar face when it turned out to be someone else altogether. One morning, she ran into the custodian at their new apartment while he swept the hallway. Startled, at first, the name stitched onto a patch on his shirt read *Gus*. He resembled her Uncle Billy to a T. It must have been true, everyone had a twin in life.

Fresh greenery graced the beds along both sides of the sidewalk leading to the main entrance to the church. Multicolored annuals sprouted between neatly trimmed barberry bushes. Some of the parishioners—the mother-daughter team of Linda and her sweet mother, Barbara—faithfully did the planting and weeding every season. Their handiwork rivaled that of a lawn and garden magazine.

"Now, don't you look pretty," said the pastor's wife to Tally as they approached the front steps to the church.

"Thank you," Tally replied. Shyly, she looked down at her feet. The child reflected a heightened sense of fashion consciousness beyond a little girl just shy of six. Becca didn't spend a lot on her clothes and often shopped at discount outlets and sometimes even the local thrift store where the gently used clothing she found was a bargain compared with the mall's prices. After raising Jason, this was her first experience with ruffles and lace, and she loved to wander through the racks of girls' dresses and outfits, especially those in bright shades of pink and yellow, which complemented Tally's honeyed-olive skin tone.

Becca smiled inside. She'd become acquainted with the generous praise her granddaughter received. Tally's well-being was Becca and Paul's highest priority, and anyone could see the child thrived in her environment, both physically and emotionally. Swim lessons, ballet, T-ball, hiking, flying kites... There was no activity unconsidered if it lent to the best for their only grandchild.

****

Margie Palmer awoke to the sound of tidewater lapping up against a dockside. Purchasing a state-of-the-art alarm clock with a virtual sound machine was her latest attempt at preserving her mind-body peace. She'd chucked her proverbial timekeeper with the obnoxious buzz a while ago and substituted one with a more soothing wake-up call that didn't jumpstart her heart. Her head half-buried in the pillow, she cracked open an eye. Early morning light framed the window's thinly slatted blinds. Traffic droned outside the window. She didn't want to face the day.

Thoughts of her dear Curt came to the forefront. A veil of sadness pressed down. The ache of his absence sunk deep into her bones. Down on herself and her life, she'd turned inward lately.

She knew she couldn't replace him, but she still held out a desperate hope of finding someone to love...one day.

Safely cocooned in the folds of a satiny pink comforter, she closed her eyes. In the pleasant virtual drift of the soothing tidewater, she went back to sleep.

At three minutes after ten, Margie awoke again. Church was already in session. Just as well. She wasn't in the mood to deal with a whole congregation of people today. After a quick shower, she pulled on a pair of black Lycra jogging pants lying on the chair where she'd strewn them the night before and picked out a fresh sweatshirt from the drawer.

The refrigerator's fruit bin held half of a leftover apple wrapped in plastic. She took it out, cut the oxidized part off, and topped it with a slice of Swiss cheese. She poured the last remains of the almond milk into a small juice glass and used it to take her vitamins.

While eating, she stared outside the kitchen window and debated whether to stay in or go out. The day beckoned. If she couldn't make church this morning, the next best place would be a walk in nature.

Chapter Eight

"How was Sunday school, baby?"

Tally cocked her head. "Fine," she replied, letting go of Becca's hand.

A flower bed caught her eye, and she kneeled in front of a tuft of sweet alyssum. She took a deep sniff of the fragrant white flowers and then scampered blithely ahead down the sidewalk again. The movement sent her ebony tresses bouncing.

"What did your teacher teach you this morning?" Paul asked when they caught up with her.

"David and Goliath," she replied, breezily, and took her grandfather's hand.

Becca gave Paul a knowing look, and he winked back at her.

Tally was in a good place. *Thank you, Lord.*

Shortly after noon, as they approached the apartment complex, Becca's cell buzzed. She fumbled for it deep inside her crowded handbag.

"Hello."

"Ms. Wallace?"

"Speaking."

"This is Holy Cross Hospital."

"Yes?" Her voice inflected higher as her nerves braced for the caller's next words.

"My son? Yes, he's Jason Wallace." Her gaze darted to Paul who stood with Tally as she busily chattered. The rest of the caller's words blurred. Becca quickly hung up and ran ahead to catch up with them. "Jason's in the hospital. He's been in an accident."

****

Margie panted heavily with every fourth stride. She jogged through pools of strangled light along the heavily shadowed path leading through Barley Hills Farm Park. Moist, leafy air filled her lungs, and a canopy of mist hovered over the path. Determined to complete the five-mile stretch of pathway, she pressed on. Normally, she traveled through this part of the park in a modest stroll, absorbed in the peaceful ambiance. It might include the little surprise of a passing rabbit's hop, or the rare glimpse of a bluebird, or even the rush of a pheasant's plumage. But today, she needed more than just a pleasant gambol. She was on a mission. She needed her life back and so picked up her pace.

The air carried a primal scent of life just waking from a winter's slumber; the bright colors of spring blooms emerged along the pathways. Fallen leaves lingered at the base of tall trees—their former gold and crimson finery now scattered to the wind—as new leaves struggled to bloom from buds studding the branches. Seeing the new life sprouting all around gave her hope that she, too, would be able to shed the doldrums of winter. No matter the season, the park, amid thick trees and winding paths, brought her thoughts captive, and the cares of life waned just a bit among the throng of birdsong and greenery.

A tiny patch of blue in the sky struggled to break free from a stretch of clouds. From this angle, the park opened up into a broad expanse of wide fields. Curt's image hovered in her mind. The last time she came here was with him. Once more, she fought off the veil of depression descending on her and pushed on.

By the time she approached the distant cornfield, her breathing labored. Her leg muscles turned rubbery, and she slowed to a walk. She kept going, not wanting to cut the outing short. This morning she needed to keep moving. Recovery from her broken heart over the past year had been slow. The searing loss of the man in her life didn't come easy. She knew God was right there with her and he held her in the palm of his hand, but she needed to do her part and "keep on keeping on" as Pastor Benson often preached.

The morning haze slowly lifted. As her breathing slowly returned to normal, thoughts of the news story about the park rapist came to mind. The perpetrator was never caught. She wondered in what part of the park the incident occurred. *Was it here?*

Water tinkled over the well-worn rocks dotting the banks of the nearby stream. Distant birds called from the trees or were fighting over the next worm. She cast her gaze in a swift 360-degree pan. Seeing nothing out of the ordinary, the sounds of nature put her mind back at ease, and she continued on the pathway as it curved along the stream through a copse of trees.

Moments later, she came up on one of the properties on the parkland—an old ramshackle building shrouded in half-light. It lent a strange presence on the bank of the creek. The roof sagged like an aging horse, and pock marks etched the front of the crumbling façade. The old building presented itself like a prop from a horror movie—a scary eyesore in the midst of an oasis. *Is anyone in there?* She never felt at ease in this part of the park because of it. Curt once told her it was where they performed experiments on people housed in the nearby sanitarium.

Margie shivered. Snippets of the Nazis' tortuous medical experiments in the concentration camps back in the mid-twentieth century during the Holocaust flashed in her head—the harrowing accounts of imprisonment in the confined barracks, along with the heart-rending stories of humiliation and egregious acts toward the unsuspecting victims. She bristled at the thought of what once may have gone on inside and picked up her pace once more.

About a hundred feet farther down the path, a strange sound came from near the creek bed. Her imagination spun with possibilities. A sick bird? A wounded fox? Someone hurt? Wherever it came from, the odd sound wasn't familiar.

Chapter Nine

The knot in Becca's stomach grew tighter as she stood in the ascending elevator at Holy Cross Hospital. She reached for Paul's hand. The elevator's *ding* sent a fresh rush of adrenaline coursing through her body.

As they passed each patient's open door, Becca couldn't divert her eyes. Her spirit ached at the sight of the bedridden. They said her son was still alive, but how bad would his injuries be? *Please God...please let my son live.*

Inside Room 337, a jagged green line etched across a black screen where a sonorous beep broke the silence. Becca rushed to her son's side.

"Jason...Jason, can you hear me?" She gently lifted his hand and held it to her face.

Paul moved to the other side of the bed and leaned in to speak. "Jason, we're here, son."

"We love you, honey," she said just above a whisper.

"You must be Mr. and Mrs. Wallace," a pleasant nurse announced upon entering the room.

Becca nodded. "Is he going to be all right?"

"How did it happen?" Paul asked.

The nurse moved to Jason's bed. "The doctor said he has a slight concussion and possibly some internal injuries and a broken wrist. Right now, we don't know for sure how extensive his injuries are, but the doctor should be able to give you all the details after the readings come back from the tests." She adjusted the wires above the bed and checked the connections of the intravenous line running into Jason's arm.

Becca's heart lodged in her throat as she watched for signs of life while he lay motionless.

****

Margie steeled herself for a moment. Where was the sound coming from? Was it human or animal? She strained to hear. Innocuous baby birds in their nests, or a duck or goose from the adjacent farm could have been squalling. Or a wildcat. She continued walking along the misty path. The sound came again. Low and muffled, the distinct cry of something emanated from somewhere by the creek below the ramshackle building. Or was it somewhere inside?

She slowly crept toward the sound and stopped just shy of an outcropping of weeds. The tangled mass of green gave her pause. *Leaves of three, let it be*. Poison Ivy. She flinched in fear of getting too close to the menacing vine.

A few yards away, a squirrel rustled among the leaves and ran off at her approach. Her focus riveted on a pile of leaves below the stone wall at the base of the old building. A piece of white cloth peeked out between the leaves. Another raspy spasm of a cry. *It's underneath the mound of leaves.* Her heart pounded as she maneuvered over the rocks onto the embankment and inched closer to the makeshift pile. Wary of exactly what made the sound, she kicked away some of the leaves and jumped back. She jolted at seeing a bloodied sheet lying there. An infant baby was wrapped inside it.

****

The hospital shone like a beacon in the distance; the face of the four-story structure glistened like a giant gemstone of blue-tinged glass. Margie waited impatiently at the traffic light. The silent drum of her fingers on the wheel was the only sound in the car as the baby stopped crying and now lay silently on the front seat.

"C'mon, already," she said through gritted teeth. She banged both hands on the wheel and then glanced at the bundle. A ripple of anxiety coursed through her as though she were on the tip of a pyramid attempting to keep her balance.

Her thrumming heart lifted as the hospital's red-and-white emergency sign came into view. Like a mouse in a maze, she raced through the parking lot and wound the car around the grassy islands and one-way signs that slowed her progress to the main entrance. Frustrated at the obstacle course of the lot's design, she silently cursed. There was no easy way to get close to the building. She picked the first open spot and wedged her car in between two SUVs. She cut the engine, scooped up the bloodied bundle, and made a dash to the emergency entrance.

A mix of anxiety and dread washed over her as she approached the automatic doors that whooshed open at her approach. At the reception desk, she stammered out the story of what happened in the park. Buoyed by her nerves, her words spilled out fast. The receptionist picked up the phone and, moments later, hospital personnel pounced through the double doors into the lobby as though a fire had just broken out.

"I'll take the baby," a red-haired triage nurse said.

The woman in white held her arms out for the tiny bundle and then rushed back inside the ER. Margie followed right behind her through the double doors. The nurse darted down the hall and placed the baby on a table in one of the examination rooms. Margie stared in fascination outside the room as the on-call doctor, along with his staff, gathered like hungry bees to honeysuckle to assist the lifeless little body. A well-run colony, they maneuvered just short of frenetic as they attended to the baby, unwrapped the bloody sheets, and checked the vital signs, all in a controlled dance of sorts while murmuring among themselves.

"We have a heartbeat," the doctor said. Margie's tension fell away. *It's alive!* Her heart swelled with relief. So many thoughts went through her head. *Whose baby is it? Is it a girl or a boy? What will become of the child—adoption or foster care?* Margie clasped her hands together and basked in the rush of it all. She'd found a baby. What were the odds? While she stood transfixed and somewhat dazed by the scene, a tall man in blue stepped through the double doors.

"Are you the woman who found the baby?"

"Yes...yes, officer." Her heart rhythm kicked up, and she wondered why a policeman would be in the emergency room talking to her. Her mind raced in a chaotic swirl of thoughts. First among them was: *Am I in trouble?*

"I have a few questions for you." He extended his arm and guided her by the elbow toward the lobby.

Chapter Ten

Becca stood at Jason's bedside. Seeing the bandages on his head and arm rocked her composure. She'd trade places if only it would spare her son any pain. Even as a little boy, she struggled to refrain from fighting his battles though her protective instincts were strong. *Don't make a sissy out of him.* Her mother's words of wisdom swam in her head.

"Jason?" She gently stroked his hand. "It's Mom." She squashed the urge to pepper him with questions about everything since he'd left home—the accident, where he was living, Lark. She restrained herself, not wanting to overwhelm him while in this state.

His eyes blinked open.

She forced a smile.

"Hey," he managed to say, groggily.

"The doctor says you have a slight concussion and a cracked rib, and you fractured your wrist. Otherwise, you'll be fine," she encouraged. "Just fine."

"So, I guess I'll live."

"Yes, of course you will." She ran her palm over his arm. "For now, just rest." She backed away from the bed and sat down on the chair by the windowsill.

"Mom?" His voice was barely above a whisper. "Is Dad here?"

"Right here, son," Paul said. He moved closer to the bed.

"I need to tell you something...both you and Mom."

Becca's curiosity sparked.

"I just—I'm...I'm just sorry—for everything."

Becca's heart softened. He'd given her and Paul so much trouble in the past, and she lived for an apology but never received any. Was he finally admitting his waywardness and owning up? Is this what it took to get justice?

Becca glanced at Paul. She didn't know whether his somber expression was from the reminder of the fire or his stepson's condition.

"I just—just wanted to—" Jason's voice broke. "I wanted you to know that I'm sorry, Dad, about the fight and everything else I screwed up."

Becca leaned over his bed and put her hand over his bandaged one.

"Jason, it's okay. For now, we just want you to focus on getting well. We can discuss the fire later. Right now, your health is more important."

"The fire destroyed half the house—" Paul began.

"Shhh, not now," she whispered. Her mood soured at the reminder of destruction the house incurred all because of her son's irresponsibility, but no matter how egregious the situation was with the house, this wasn't the time or place to discuss it.

"We tried reaching you, but your voicemail was full," Paul said.

"No, it wasn't full. It wasn't even set up yet," Becca countered.

"Same thing," he mumbled.

Becca braced for the worst. This wasn't the best time to bring up her son's shortcomings, and she didn't mean to castigate him—not now. Yet, here they were, wading into the swamp.

In her heart, she struggled with the idea that Jason started the fire in the basement. How could he be capable of such retribution? She knew his drug habits were serious and he was receiving counseling for his behavior and bad choices, but the situation with the fire left her flummoxed. It didn't sound like her Jason, but maybe his mind had snapped.

Jason's eyes fluttered open. He gazed at her intently, eyes beseeching.

"Wait. What are you talking about? A fire? I don't understand," he uttered, hoarsely. "I didn't start any fire." His voice strained. "I'm sorry for wrecking the car and...for, well, being a selfish jerk, I'll admit all of that. But what's this about a fire?"

"You didn't start the fire in your room downstairs?" she said, puzzled. "Because your father kicked you out of the house and you were upset and..." She let her words ebb as her heart vacillated between despair and relief.

Jason slowly shook his head, his face forlorn. "No, I didn't. I could never do that to you and Dad."

Becca let his words settle. The room grew silent with the weight of them. Jason's expression resembled the mirror image of when he was a young child, the time she blamed him for eating the last of the cupcakes. Turned out Paul ate them. She batted away her negative thoughts hovering repellently in the web of her mind. The innocence her son held in his beleaguered eyes softened any ill will she held inside. Her heart lifted.

Becca and Paul locked eyes. The tension in his face remained, but he held a glimmer of hope in his eyes as though something melted within. She could tell they were both sharing the same struggle. *Was this really true?*

Chapter Eleven

Becca paced up and down Jason's bedside. Her thoughts turned to her son as a little boy and his desire to play with matches; though he never started a deliberate fire as far as she knew. His ninth-grade teacher once recommended counseling for his occasional bursts of temper. She didn't hesitate in agreeing with the woman about getting him the necessary help. Becca's guilt at thinking she was a bad parent fueled her desire to intervene in Jason's well-being going forward. If counseling was what he needed, then she saw that he received as much as he could.

Becca turned to Jason again and just above a whisper said, "Jason?"

Silence.

"Honey?"

Jason stirred. His eyes flitted open and then closed. He made a guttural sound that didn't sound coherent.

Paul folded his arms across his chest. "Looks like his sedatives pulled him under again."

"Jason?" Becca leaned closer to his bed. "Jason, can you hear me?"

They waited. Paul glanced at his watch. "He's out. I think we should just let him sleep, Bec."

"Okay, but just a few more minutes." She stood by his bed and waited for him to rouse again.

Outside the door in the hallway, two figures in lab coats spoke in hushed tones. They could have been psychologists. Shrinks were all part of the same clinical parade of starchy white-coated, bald and bespectacled men, who marched around with their yellow notepads tucked under their arms—only lately, they came with an electronic variety. The white lab coats they wore lent an air of authority that brought Becca back to the first psychologist she ever met...

...Becca hated being taken out of her sixth-grade class and thought something was wrong with her after the fight with her classmate, Sheryl Dunbar. The school counselor studied Becca behind his wire rims as though she were a rare specimen under a microscope of judgment and discrimination, while he mentally poked further into her mind as though mining for gold. He didn't find much and concluded she was just a normal kid...

Not so for Jason. He'd been labeled a problem child early on. She'd sympathized with his angst during his rebellious years after she'd left his father and harbored guilt as he underwent the same type of probing—peppered with countless questions, first by school counselors and later by prison psychologists. They wanted to help, but the consensus was that he was afraid of being helped. It would mean giving up the substances that masked the pain and being forced to carry the burden alone. *Juvenile delinquent* was the label scrawled on his case record, and he wouldn't be changing anytime soon. That's what all of the counselors thought. Becca's heart broke that her son might always be this way.

****

Becca ran her hand along Jason's bedrail. The intermittent beep of the monitors and blinking lights didn't make sense...101, 112, 98... *Was a higher number better than lower?* The colors and variations of statistics were beyond her medical understanding. At one point, the machine's innocuous beeping turned shrill. Her heart lurched. *Should the nurse be alerted?* Before she uttered a word, Jason's nurse hastened into the room.

"It's fine. It sometimes does this." The nurse adjusted something and left as quickly as she came in.

Relieved, Becca put her hand on Jason's bandaged arm and rubbed her thumb on the rough cloth holding his bones together. *Please heal him, Lord.* In the semi-quiet of the room, she reached for Paul's hand. He moved closer and wrapped his arm around her. She ached for her son's bedridden situation and all he'd endured over the years. Her thoughts turned back to the last time she felt this way...

...They watched through a mirrored window. The practice was not commonplace at the prison, but the officials made an exception for them since they had connections; a relative, once removed, on Paul's side of the family was a high-ranking member of the prison board.

Jason sat on a wooden chair. The wobbly legs rocked audibly whenever he shifted his weight. The desk in front of him, clear of any clutter, held only an old-fashioned, landline telephone. The expression on his face told her his psyche had calloused over and he was numb to his surroundings. Becca hoped he hadn't forgotten the sweetness of freedom outside the prison walls in the rolling hills of Pennsylvania, along with his family who needed him. Her heart tore at seeing her son in the room...in this predicament...the wages of his addiction.

Jason made fists behind his back waiting for the doctor. As far as she knew, he would hate the probing questions. But the time he spent with the psychologist was far better than sitting in the hot, dank jail cell, a break from the routine of the empty gray walls.

"Hello, Jason." The doctor lent a professional smile as she stepped into the room. A pretty blonde, she took a seat across from him and cupped her hands together. "I'm Dr. Hollister." She paused. "But you may call me Molly." She opened the manila file folder in front of her. "I want to ask you some questions." She gave a polite nod as though underscoring her purpose. "I'm curious here." She focused on the paperwork. "You had a falling out with your father some time ago." She readjusted her glasses and peered up at him. "Is this correct?"

Becca flinched at the doctor's words. Jason hadn't mentioned much of his father in a long time. Why dwell on a dead man?

Jason shifted, obviously uncomfortable with the question. He wiped his face with the back of his hand.

Dr. Hollister leaned back in her swivel chair and steepled her fingers. "Talk to me about you father."

Jason squirmed. "My father?" He gave her a puzzled look. "What's there to talk about? I mean what do you want to know?"

"Well, let's start with your relationship. Was he a good father, would you say?"

"Ahhh, no," Jason shook his head. "No, not a good father."

"How was he not a good father?"

Jason ran his palm across his bristled face. "Ah, let's see. You wanna list or something?"

She replied, "Any way you want to tell me is your choice."

"Okay, um, well, he was a jerk to my mother, I remember," he said. "And I once saw him beat her with his belt when I was like five or six."

Becca cringed. In her heart, she'd always been concerned whether he witnessed his father's bullying toward her. Jason never mentioned anything to her about it and apparently kept his thoughts inside. She braced for what he'd say next.

The doctor crossed her arms low at her waistline. "How did you respond?"

"Respond?" He stifled a chuckle. "I was a kid. How was I supposed to *respond*?" He shook his head. "I dunno how I responded, I just told you that I saw it, is all."

"Okay, continue," she encouraged.

"And, I guess, that's when she left him or soon did. And took me with her."

"I see." She typed something onto her laptop. "Now, when was the last time you saw him—was it then, as a little boy?"

Jason chewed the inside of his cheek and cast his eyes down at the floor before answering. "I didn't see him much until later."

"Later, as in—?"

"Like when I was a teenager." He shifted in his chair. "He stayed in touch—you know, on and off through the years. Until my mom got married again."

"Some people would be upset about that. Were you?"

He shrugged. "I was okay with it." He nodded his approval. "My stepdad was a lot better than my biological one, that's for sure."

Becca squeezed Paul's hand. "He's got that right," she whispered.

Paul nodded, still focused on the window.

"Did your father have any problem with her getting remarried?"

"My father?" He shrugged. "I don't know. Don't think so. The cards stopped. I guess he lost contact with her."

"So, how did you two reconnect later, as you mentioned?"

Becca sat riveted and hung on his words.

"It was up in the mountains in Kempton." He blew out a breath. "I'd been helping out part-time at this lodge and campground, tending the barn, mowing the lawn. An old friend of the family owned the area. He'd been sick. Sclerosis of the liver, or something, and Mom said it might be a nice way to help him and his wife."

"So, go on...about your father."

"One day, he was just there. Like he appeared out of nowhere."

"How did you take it? Happy...sad?"

Jason shook his head. "I didn't think much about it."

"Not at all?"

"I mean, I hadn't seen him in years. We all thought he'd passed away from alcohol poisoning or something." He ran his hand down the back of his head. "He drank a lot."

"What happened next?"

Jason paused and appeared to be deep in thought. He ran his palm across his face. Becca held her breath.

"I don't want to talk about it!" he barked in a decibel overload.

Doctor Hollister's kind eyes enlarged behind her glasses. She whipped the spectacles off and placed them in her lab coat pocket.

"Jason," she said. Her eyes locked with his. "You'll be released on parole in a couple of weeks. Your *parole*...this is a good thing. You'll be able to go back home. I just want you to make every effort to transition well."

He averted his gaze from the psychiatrist, and Becca knew he wouldn't say anything more. The boy—and now the man—could never be forced out of his shell once he climbed inside. It would take a very special person to pry him out. Talking about the man was like dredging an abyss so deep, who knew what was inside? While he may have been hiding something, she didn't blame him. She'd spent the better part of eighteen years trying to do the same thing. Escaping the memories of her past was how she coped...

****

As Jason slept, Becca and Paul stood shoulder-to-shoulder and prayed silently at their son's bedside. Their hearts were burdened for his healing—both physically and in every other way.

"Love you, Jas," Becca said. She kissed his bandaged head.

Paul leaned over and laid his hand on Jason's shoulder. "Get well, son."

Chapter Twelve

Uplifted by the morning's events, Margie walked on air as she left the hospital. She barely felt the cushioned insoles of her running shoes on the way to the parking lot. *I found a baby!*

Her joy must have been contagious, as the first person who passed her in the lot smiled in her direction. Could they feel her joy? Despite her over-the-top contentment, the mental and physical ordeal from the morning's events left her drained. A gaping hole of hunger gnawed. As she made her way to her car at the lower end of the lot, she was pleasantly surprised to see the familiar figure of her friend Becca and her husband.

"Becca, Paul!" She hastened toward them. The Wallaces pivoted in unison as she approached. "Hey,"—she put her hand on her hip—"what are you guys doing here?" Before they could answer, she blurted out, "I just delivered a baby!" At the same time, a Medivac helicopter hovered over the roof of the hospital where it prepared for landing.

"Jason," Becca replied over the din of noise overhead. She held her ears as the *clop-clop* of the swirling rotors of the helicopter fluttered above.

Margie figured by their sober expressions that they didn't hear what she had said over the noise.

Parallel lines drew between Becca's eyes. "He was in an accident at work."

"Fell from a ladder, they told us," Paul explained. His dour expression matched Becca's.

Margie slumped her shoulders at the news. "No!"

"But he'll be all right." Becca gave a short affirmative nod. "The doctor confirmed it's a concussion with a few broken bones...something about his spleen maybe, they're not sure, and the need for some minor surgery at some point, but thankfully, nothing too serious."

"Oh, for heaven's sake." Margie glanced back at the hospital. "Poor Jason, I'm so sorry to hear this. But it's great news he'll be okay."

Becca nodded.

"Kids heal fast."

"I hope. Hey, wait. Did you mention a baby or something before?"

Margie grinned. "Uh-huh." She clasped her hands together, carried away by her own ebullience. "I feel so maternal."

"Don't tell us you *had* a baby," Becca giggled. "I just saw you last week, and you didn't look the slightest bit with child."

"Well, you could say that. Because it's true!" Margie's voice escalated. "I *found* a baby!"

"What?" Becca's eyes popped.

"At Barley Hills Park, right near that old dilapidated building"—her words tumbled out fast—"off the path by the old baseball field." Margie twisted around and signaled the direction of where it had happened. "By that old white shack, the one where we thought they kept the insane, remember?"

"How in the world?" Becca's mouth hung agape. "I've heard of people doing that before—finding a baby. I read online once that someone found one under the tire of a car. But still, it's just so crazy."

Margie recited her morning foray into the woods and laid out every detail right through to the words of the doctor when they found the baby still alive.

"Just wow," Becca exclaimed. "That trail always gave me the creeps when we used to go there with Jason and his buddy, Trey, when they were children. Even you and I." She glanced at Paul. "We went there a lot when we were first married." She paused.

"And last summer someone was attacked." She shivered, mockingly and turned to Margie. "Did you hear about it?"

"Yeah, but today's Sunday. I figured what bad can come on the Lord's day, right?" She shrugged. "All the bad guys were out late last night and probably still sleeping."

"You're a brave one, Margie," Paul said. "Was there anyone else around?"

"Nope, just me and the squirrels." *And a sweet little baby.*

An image of Curt popped into her mind and how they had tried so hard to conceive. Now, having to give the baby away, it was as though the Lord didn't want her to have children at all.

"Too wild." Becca clasped her hands together. "I can't get over it. You must have been blown away."

"Tell me about it," she said. "So, then this cop comes into the hallway and stops in front of me. He looks like a linebacker." She drew her hands out wide. "He asked me if I'd been the one who found the baby. Said he wanted to speak with me, and he's checking me out like I was a freak or something." She rolled her eyes. "At least, that's how I felt. But then he turned out to be cool. He understood. Now that I think about it, he probably was right to be skeptical. Who knows these days, right? It could have been just a scam from some crazy woman." She held her hand up. "Don't say it. I know, I know, I am crazy, but..."

They both smiled.

"Hey, I'm starved. You guys had lunch yet? There's a new restaurant at the mall I've been meaning to try. Has organic soups and everything." Margie tapped a finger to her forehead. "Oh, what is the name of that place?" she mumbled under her breath.

"Oh, Marg, we'd love to, but we left Tally with our neighbor." Becca's mouth drew down. "I'd hate to take advantage of the poor woman."

"Hey, not a problem. We'll catch up next time."

"We will, Margie, definitely." Becca nodded.

"Okay then," she replied with a wave. "See y'all later."

Margie headed down Row E back to her car. The cavernous hole of hunger in her stomach grew as she pulled out of the parking lot. The mall was several miles away, and spotting a burger joint sign on the right up ahead, she quickly changed her mind. The vision of a ketchup-mustard-pickle-onion burger with fries beckoned.

****

Images of food in perfect lighting turned everything on the menu board into ambrosia as the warm scent of hot fryer grease permeated the air. Margie perused the menu selections. Her mouth salivated. She practically lived on fast food; though, lately, she had become interested in the latest medical information on health food, and articles about how fake the food was becoming—now dubbed *Frankenfood*—and other toxic things flooded her email and Facebook newsfeed regularly. It seemed the more she took the click-bait, the more stories appeared. Today, she put all of it out of her mind. Her stomach begged for carbs and fat.

One person stood ahead of her in line—a heavy-set woman in a denim jacket. The woman placed her order and then moved to the side while chatting on her cell. Margie stepped up and requested a hamburger, small salad, and a diet Coke. While the woman continued talking, there was something familiar about her voice.

Margie picked up her food and stopped at the utensil station before heading back to the car. To her, everything tasted better outside, and she could barely wait to eat. Before she turned to leave, she heard someone call her name.

"Margie?" The denim-clad woman ahead of her in line stared directly at Margie, an inkling of a curious smile spread on her lips.

Chapter Thirteen

Margie stopped short. *Who is this person?* Obviously, the woman knew her. An old work associate? Someone from high school, middle school, or her childhood neighborhood? Her head swam.

"Hey," the woman said, grinning.

Embarrassed, Margie tried to hide her inability to place the woman.

"Hi," Margie said, keeping a friendly air.

"How you doing, girl?"

Margie nodded, still struggling and hoped her mind would snap into gear fast. "Um...oh, wait. *Alena*?"

"*Athena*," the woman corrected. She flashed a broad smile punctuated by a gold tooth.

"A-*theen*-a," Margie pronounced with emphasis. "Yes, how could I forget?"

Her thoughts reverted back to her first job out of college. She had begun a social work career at the Family Hope and Healing Agency in Philadelphia, and Athena and her granddaughter were among her first clients. She remembered the little girl being wild and full of life. Margie loved all of her assigned children, and they were all adorable in their own way, but the beauty and energy of Athena's granddaughter put her in a different league.

The warm, salty aroma of comfort food wafted from the bag. Margie's stomach rumbled. She mentally debated whether to keep the conversation short and sweet or sit down at the table and chat with the woman. She could linger for a minute, but was she obligated to eat with her? At this point, there was no tactful way short of a lie to get out of it. Without a reason to bolt—except for selfishly wanting a Sunday afternoon alone—she re-thought the situation. Maybe this was some kind of divine appointment? Working with Pastor Benson for so long, she'd heard him preach on the topic on more than one occasion. His words rang in her head. *Man plans his way, but the Lord directs his steps.*

"Come sit with me," Athena said. She moved the box of chicken wings and soda off to the side to make some space. "Here"— she patted the table— "got plenty of room, c'mon."

Margie, still drifting on a happy wave from what transpired earlier that morning, resigned herself to stay.

"So, what you got there?" Athena grasped a french fry and pointed to the bag with it.

Margie drew out the salad first and plopped it down.

"That all you got?" she said. "A dang ol' salad?"

Margie held up the burger. "This, too."

"Have a chicken nugget, girl." She shoved the box across the table.

Margie smiled inside. Apparently, Athena didn't notice Margie's true size underneath the sweatpants. "Need to watch what I eat these days." She ducked her head and lent a contrite smile.

"Bah," Athena said with a dismissive wave of her wrist laced in bling. "Life's too short." She chomped down on a chicken nugget and through a mouthful asked, "So, what'cha been doing with yourself all these years?"

Margie hesitated over where to begin. She shared about her beloved Curt and glossed over much of everything else. Athena listened and then shared her own past stories and anecdotes.

At one point after chatting for a while, Margie glanced down at the table. All that was left of her lunch were a few sesame seeds lingering in the middle of the wrapper and a wilted piece of lettuce in the salad bowl. She was full but barely remembered eating. The savory part was lost in conversation.

Margie glanced around the restaurant. At the next table, a couple and two children sat chomping down on their burgers, chased by milkshakes and sodas. She envied seeing them relish their food sans chitchat.

"So, I see you been doing well for yourself, Miss Margie," Athena said in mid-chew. Her words drew Margie's attention back. "So sorry to hear about your dear husband, though." She shook her head and popped another chicken nugget into her mouth. "Uh-huh. War sure is a terrible thing."

Athena listened and nodded in the dance of sympathetic understanding and then reached for her cell phone.

"Gotta show you my pictures." Athena focused on the screen; her long fire-engine-red fingernail tapped page after page as she scrolled through the queue of pictures.

Margie hated waiting while people flipped through their pictures. She mentally rolled her eyes. *You're in for the duration.* She longed for another burger.

"Oh, here," Athena said, brightening. "Here's a picture of my granddaughter now."

In the glare of the light streaming in through the window, Margie craned her neck. "Ah, yes, she's all grown up." She smiled, admiringly. "Still cute."

Athena nodded. "Yep, sure is. That's my baby."

"Who's that with her?" Margie pointed to a man who stood next to her. "Her husband?"

Athena licked the salt from her lips. "Oh, no, no. That's... um...you know, I don't know his name now. Isn't that funny?" She pulled the phone back and continued scrolling. "Okay, now here's a picture of my *great*-granddaughter."

Margie leaned in again to view the photo. "Oh, she's quite the cutie, too."

"Yes," Athena agreed. "Looks just like her mama, don't you think?"

"Yes, very much so."

"I love that li'l one. My Tally." She glanced back at Margie and said, "I'd kill for her," before a broad smile slipped onto her face and quickly faded like raindrops in a desert.

Chapter Fourteen

"There's a court case on the fourteenth of August. My attorney just called and faxed me the notice from Child Protective Services."

"What time?" Pastor Benson asked.

"Ten-thirty. It's a Tuesday. I hope it's a good day for you."

Becca didn't want to put him out, but if anyone could vouch for her and Paul's integrity as fit parents for Tally, it would be the pastor.

"Looks good from here," he replied.

"Great, it's at the courthouse on School Street."

"Yes, I'm familiar with it."

"Thanks, Pastor."

"And now it's on my calendar. Oh, and Becca, I just want to encourage you not to worry. I know it's not easy, but this is for the Lord to deal with. Just give it to him."

"I know, sir. I'm trying to keep a level head about it."

"All right then, we'll be praying. See you soon."

Becca hung up with the pastor as the doorbell rang. Through the peephole stood Jane, her old neighbor. "Jane!" Becca exclaimed as she opened the door.

"Hey, there," Jane replied in her all-too-cute southern twang, a Macy's shopping bag at her side. Her signature scent wafted in.

"Come on in, lady." She took a step back. "Welcome to our downsized abode."

Jane lifted the bag with two hands. "Got some of your stuff here."

"Oh, let me take that." Becca pried the handles from her. "Whoa, heavy. What's in here?"

"You lent me a lot over the years. I had no idea how much until I started cleaning out my drawers and closets. I found your lantern, roasting pan, knife sharpener, and some books."

Becca put the bag down. "Oh, you could have kept the books," she said with a dismissive wave. "How many times can I read Barbara Taylor Bradford?" *Actually, her books are pretty good if the Queen of England endorsed her.*

"No, no." Jane shook her head. "I've been on the losing end of things not returned to me enough. I didn't want to do it to someone else."

Becca sat down on the sofa. "Have a seat, I have something to tell you." She picked up the notification letter and dangled it in front of her.

"What's that?"

"Court hearing." Her lips drew tight. "And I'm nervous."

"What for?" Jane took a seat beside her.

"Custody." She shook her head. "Just don't know how it's going to turn out."

"You've been the primary caretaker, the...um, what is it, foster something?"

"Foster Kinship."

"Right. So, what's the problem? You've had custody for over a year now."

"Over two," Becca corrected. "Almost *three*."

"Okay, then. She's practically adopted as it is. I mean, she's with you and Paul most of the time, right?"

"Actually, she goes to the other grandmother—really, her *great*-grandmother, every other week or so for weekend visits." She rolled her eyes. "When the woman is lucid." Becca made a face. "She's not very responsible."

Jane gave her a questioning look. "That's not even close to what you do."

"I know. But still, I'm worried."

"Well, you shouldn't be, Becca." She waved the air. "Hey, if you need me for anything, I'm available."

Becca brightened. "You know, that would be great because I really do need your help. Can you be one of my witnesses? Vouch for me and Paul to be *suitable*"—she made air quotes— "parents and all?"

"Absolutely," Jane exclaimed. "I'd love to. Count me in."

"Thanks. I can use as much ammunition as I can muster."

Chapter Fifteen

Becca studied herself in the full-length mirror.

"Hon, I wish I could be there today," Paul said. His puppy dog eyes hung sadly.

"I know." She adjusted her skirt. "It's okay."

Paul slipped on his belt and tightened it to the third notch. "I feel guilty."

"You have a commitment to your work. It's fine, really. It's not like I'll be alone. I've got the others and the pastor. I'll be okay."

"Galls me that the summer school's final exam is today. Of all days."

"Paul, you're the proctor. You have to be there." She patted his arm. "Not to worry. I'll give you the lowdown tonight." As she put her shoes on, Becca heard a soft knock at the door. "Oh, that's Miss Bea. I'll get it."

Becca slipped on her wedding ring and then ran down the hall. She checked the peep hole and found the diminutive woman standing there wearing a yellow sarong skirt with a white blouse and ballet flats. *Always on time.*

"Morning, Miss Bea," Becca greeted, warmly.

"Yes, yes," she replied, nodding. "Good morning."

"Thank you for coming over today. We appreciate you watching Tally for us."

"Yes, yes, not problem, Ms. Wallace. Tally is wonderful child."

"Miss Bea," exclaimed Tally, who ran up the hallway into the room. "Come see my new dolls." She grabbed the woman by the hand and nearly yanked her from the spot where she stood. "I'll show you."

"Hold on, Tal," Becca said in a half-apology to Miss Bea. She gave Tally a disapproving look. "I need to talk to Miss Bea first. After I leave, you can have her all to yourself, okay?"

Tally, still holding Miss Bea's hand, grinned ear-to-ear.

****

The morning sky hung in a milky white haze as Becca pulled into the long, winding driveway of Children's Court and navigated her way around the parking lot. She pulled into a space under a large shade tree. Perspiration gathered under her arms from her wracked nerves. The humidity didn't help. She cringed at the thought of her only silk-blend ivory blouse staining and quickly pulled out a tissue and blotted the excess moisture. Tendrils from her upswept French knot hung loosely around her face and, fortunately, her lightly applied mineral make-up remained in place and hadn't melted as she checked herself in her compact mirror. Her stomach cinched. *Deep breath, Becca,* she told herself. *Just breathe.* The clock read twenty-one minutes after ten. Nine minutes to showtime.

After a quick prayer, she stepped out of the car. The warm, close air clung sheath-like around her as she made her way toward the imposing granite-colored building. In roughly ten minutes, she'd meet her fate, if they kept to the predetermined schedule. She believed with certainty that the court wanted the best interests for the children and, in her case, they would see how well Tally thrived under her and Paul's supervision. Surely, her granddaughter was happy living with them, and everyone knew it. Becca brought three witnesses to prove her case, plus a lawyer.

Becca pictured herself standing before the judge. Since the day the notice arrived from the County regarding the custody hearing, she practiced what she would say. She chose her words carefully and was determined not to appear too cavalier or, even worse, too desperate. Even after days of delivering her plea in front of a mirror, the thought of appearing before the judge remained a sticking point. The weight of the moment pressed down on her. Even with the guidance of her lawyer, Tony Perez, along with the support of Pastor Benson and her two closest friends, this moment was as daunting as walking on a balance beam. She feared what would happen if she fell, but if God were with her, the court session would, hopefully, go according to plan. Tally would have a permanent, loving home with two stable grandparents and no more shuttling between homes like an aimless vagabond. Becca was sure God wanted what was best for Tally as much as she and Paul.

People milled in clusters around the front of the building; some puffed nervously on cigarettes while others chatted with associates or lawyered up with their well-heeled attorneys. She quickly spotted Pastor Benson, who stood by the flagpole. He wore a sharp navy sport coat and light khaki dress pants. Margie, who stood next to with him in a casual tulip-pink sheath dress and low-heeled black pumps, waved from across the courtyard. Becca's insides fluttered as she waved back.

"Where's Paul?" Margie asked as Becca approached.

"Oh, he's needed at the school today." Becca scrunched her face into a modest frown. "He planned on being here. Bummer, right?"

"Well, we're here." Pastor Benson lent a confident smile. "You all set?" He gently patted her forearm.

Becca nodded.

"Yes, you'll do fine."

"Yep, I'm good, just waiting for my attorney." She glanced around the courtyard as her stomach did the butterfly dance. "And my friend Jane from my old neighborhood said she'd be here." She turned around as a tiny figure dressed in a bright yellow sundress appeared from the side of the building. "Oh, here she is." With nervous energy bubbling, Becca gave a tiny wave as the woman approached the group. "Hey, girl." Becca hugged her and turned toward the others. "Jane, this is Pastor Benson and my friend, Margie, from church."

"Hi, there," Jane replied with her sweet southern charm. "Pleasure to meet y'all."

Margie nodded and Pastor smiled broadly, extending his hand.

"I'm so excited," Jane gushed. "I've never been to a hearing."

"Neither have I," Margie replied. She waved her hand in front of her glistening face.

Pastor tapped the face of his sleek silver watch. "It's almost ten-thirty. We should probably head inside now."

Becca's stomach did another little dance as she trailed behind the others across the courtyard with Pastor leading the way. She absently ran her hand along her pearl necklace and shot a furtive glance around the courtyard as she stood in the queue leading to the front door.

"Has anyone seen my lawyer, Tony?"

Margie turned around. "I'm sure he'll be here," she encouraged with a nod.

Becca's tension held fast like the feeling before giving a stage performance. A flush of nervous energy rose in her chest as she followed them until she paused at seeing her lawyer hastening toward her.

"Tony! Oh, thank God. I was so worried." Becca let go of her necklace and wrapped her arms around him.

"Sorry, was stuck waiting for a funeral procession, and then I couldn't find a space to park." He half-turned and signaled toward the parking area. "It's wall-to-wall cars. I had to park on the other side of the building around back." Beads of sweat gathered above his thick black eyebrows. His tawny face shone like a bronzed god in the morning sun.

"It's all good." Becca gave him tight smile. Her pastor's words echoed: *God has this...not to worry.*

After passing through the initial checkpoint where the uniformed authorities presented themselves so staunch and imposing in their crisp white shirts and creased black pants, Becca begrudgingly placed her leather bag on the x-ray conveyor belt. She inwardly flinched and wondered how many germs were coating the worn surface, hating to watch her personal effects depart from her sight to disappear inside the tunnel—even for a minute.

Becca stepped through the scanner adjacent to the x-ray conveyor belt and expected to pick up her bag at the other end. To her surprise, an armed security guard with blue latex gloves had already retrieved her Coach bag and had opened it. In his hand was a pair of cuticle nippers. A curious look emerged on his face.

Oh, boy. Here we go.

The guard asked, "What are these?" as though they were poison.

"Oh, those are for my nails," she said, unapologetically.

"You'll have to take these out, ma'am. I'm sorry."

Half-jaw scissors? They can barely remove the skin of the cuticle, the job they were designed to perform.

"Where do want me to put them?"

"You can take them to your car," the young man replied.

Becca audibly sighed. "I'll need my purse, sir. My keys are inside." She pointed to her bag.

Perturbed by the ludicrous threat her scissors posed, she took her handbag and the nail kit and marched out the door.

On her way back into the building to join her team, she first peeked inside the main holding room, now filled to capacity with expectant hopefuls awaiting their court cases.

"No seats," Becca announced as she approached the group. She folded her arms across her chest. "We'll have to wait here, I guess." Her feet ached in the high heels she wore and felt like overpacked pork rolls in too-tight casing. In an effort to ease her discomfort, she leaned against the wall and alternated standing on one foot to give the other one a rest.

Becca studied the people entering and exiting Courtroom A-3. She nibbled on a fingernail already bitten down to a nub and mentally counted the minutes before she'd enter the courtroom. Margie came and stood beside her.

"It must be past your court time by now."

"I know. I hate waiting."

Pastor frowned as he looked at his watch.

Becca scanned the interior of the holding room where wall-to-wall people murmured in hushed tones, their faces stoic. Young, old, black, white, every demographic represented. To think these folks were all here for one basic reason: love for their children. Her heart tore at the situation at hand. Sadly, it took a court to decide the future for all of them.

"I hope this starts soon." Becca bit her lip. "These heels." She grimaced, annoyed with her choice of footwear. "I should have worn flats." She silently berated herself for keeping up appearances. Who really cared whether she was fashionable? Her love for Tally was the determining factor in all of this. No one would be looking at her shoes, at least no one who held power in the court case proceedings.

"Hang in there, Bec," Jane said, as she swept the platinum bangs out of her eyes.

Becca reached down to rub her heel. Jane's beige wedges looked invitingly comfortable, and Becca wished she could have traded shoes, not to mention places with Jane. She and her husband had nary a problem in the world as Becca saw it. Not having kids was the primary reason, she supposed. Still, she envied the woman's slim figure and also her lovely house—the one next-door to her half-burnt pile of rafters and shingles that could not be fixed short of a razing and rebuilding project. She and Paul decided the expense would be too much for them to handle.

"I'm going for a walk." Becca nodded toward the hallway. "Be right back."

She headed past the holding room and around the corner where a long hall held a number of conference rooms. Farther down, a line of women queued up at the ladies' room. Midway down the hall, Margie's voice called out behind her. "Right behind you, Bec."

Becca turned and pointed ahead. "The ladies' room is down here on the left."

As she passed the conference room, something caught her attention. She double backed her steps and took a closer look inside the glass window.

She froze. "What the...I can't believe it," Becca said, her voice a notch above a whisper.

"What is it?"

"My daughter-in-law is in there."

"Your daughter-in-law?"

"Yep. And her grandmother."

"What's she doing here?"

Becca shuddered. She never wanted anyone to know that Lark had been involved in the drug world. It was bad enough her son carried the reputation. Now that the truth was out, there was nothing more to hide. A sense of liberation, of sorts, settled inside her. "Apparently, they let her out for the hearing."

Margie pressed in beside her and peered inside. "Look, there's shackles on her feet. So barbaric. What'd she do to end up in prison?"

Becca hesitated to reply. But there was nowhere to go with the blunt question.

"Drugs. Same as Jason."

"Selling or using?"

"Both, I guess. I don't really know all of the gruesome details." She paused. "I'd rather not know." *Less to explain to Tally when she comes of age.*

"Sad." Margie shook her head and then looked back into the conference room. "Wait a second. Is that *Athena*?"

"Who? Did you say, *Athena?* How do you know Athena?"

"When I was a social worker in Philly, years ago." Margie stared through the conference room window. The elderly woman sat across the table from a younger woman and their caseworker, a man in a suit. "So, that must be Lark. Wow. I remember her from ages ago when she was a little thing. She and Athena came to my agency, Hope and Healing." She paused. "So that's who Jason married..." her words drifted. Margie continued staring. "Hey. You know, that guy looks familiar."

"Which one?"

"The guy in the lit-up tie." A tall, dark man in a smart navy pinstripe and a bold yellow power tie sat at the table across from Athena.

"The yellow one?"

"Uh-huh."

"It's probably Lark's caseworker."

"Looks like the guy in the picture," Margie mused.

"What picture?"

"The one Athena showed me on her I-phone."

"When was this?"

"A couple of months ago I ran into her when I stopped for lunch—the day I found the baby in the park." Margie pulled her eyes away from the window and said in a serious tone, "I think he had his arm around Lark in the picture, or they were just standing very close together."

"Are you sure, Margie?" Becca flushed, blindsided by Margie's revelation. A surge of irritation welled.

"I'm pretty sure it was, but I could be wrong."

"You mean, like they were just posing for a picture, or?"

"*Or.*" Margie frowned. "It looked—well, it seemed like they were *together.*"

Chapter Sixteen

Becca paced outside the door of Courtroom A-3. Her heels clicked on the polished floor, and her feet—scrunched inside high heels all morning—throbbed. The perspiration under her arms gravitated now to her palms. *What is holding this thing up?*

In light of what Margie told her, adding to her simmering pressure, Becca seethed inside with the presumption her daughter-in-law had not been faithful to her son. She believed Margie and what she saw. Pictures don't lie. Now, she had all the more reason to demand custody of Tally. Neither her out-of-work, hospitalized son nor his floozy of a wife had the financial means nor the substance of good parents. The situation was an open-and-shut case.

The narrow hall outside the courtrooms flooded with a wave of people coming and going. Pastor Benson stood quietly off to the side—a fixture of calmness amid the bustle, while Tony studied a folder containing a stack of papers like he was cramming for a mid-term exam. A guard stood barking orders to keep the area clear as though it was hazardous to linger. His words didn't make much of an impression to the crowd that shuffled along like a restless tide. A man in a suit sidled up to Tony, and they shared a few words before the man stepped away.

"Becca," called Tony. He beckoned with his hand at the threshold to the holding room.

A wave of anxiety coursed its way through her loins. *Lord, stay with me.*

"Is it time yet?" She pointed to her wrist. She didn't wear her watch today, but her gut told her more than enough time had passed.

"Listen, I have some bad news." A beleaguered expression creased his bronzed face.

"What is it?" Becca's stomach dropped.

"I'm sorry, but it looks like there won't be any witnesses allowed in the courtroom today."

"What?" she cried. "Why not?"

"Just got word from one of the staff."

She shot a glance at the crowd pressing in all around. Sharply cut suits milled back and forth. Rolex watches flashed. A thick scent of amber-tinged cologne lingered in the wake of attorneys, who, along with the personnel from Youth Services, stood out from everyone else like neon signs. Which one of them laid down the gauntlet? The caseworker Darrell Harding? Maybe his supervisor? Of course, it was most likely Judge Lazinsky, the toughest one in the county, she heard, who made the decision.

Saddened by the snubbing of her efforts to support her case, her mood plummeted, and a stab of guilt hit for wasting everyone's time. Her friends stood chatting across the room, none the wiser. Now, she'd have to give them the news.

As though Margie had radar, she glanced up and caught Becca's eye. A moment later, both she and Jane hastened across the lobby floor, along with Pastor Benson.

"Hey, guys," Becca began in a dour tone. "Bad news. Tony just told me you won't be able to go in."

"Why?" Margie's face morphed into regret. "What happened?"

"Oh, no." Jane's features fell.

"Sorry, ladies." Tony shrugged. "It'll be just me—this time. Maybe in the future—"

"Hold on. What?" Becca's pulse ticked up a notch. "You mean *them*, right?"—she pointed to her friends—"*I* can go in, just not them, is that what you mean?"

Tony scratched his neck and shook his head.

"You've got to be kidding," Becca shot back. A flush of heat rose up the back of her neck.

He shifted the papers under his arm to the other. "Tough break." He patted her shoulder. "But all's not lost. I'll take care of things."

Her spirit broke. She cast her gaze to the floor, feeling as though God had left her out on a limb and withdrew his support. Her efforts and the ammunition she had cobbled together in the form of her friends' testimonies to add along with her lawyer's to make her case cut and dried were all for naught. She had solid proof and four witnesses to support her cause. They'd vouch for her and Paul and make them look golden in comparison to Athena, who didn't have a spouse and lived on the wrong side of the tracks. Now, it would be Tony's testimony alone. Becca silently cursed the situation.

On the verge of tears, she glanced over at Courtroom A-3 as the door burst open and people from the earlier court session filed out. She took a step back to let them pass as Tony pressed forward on the other side of the queue. He held his hand against door. "I won't let you down, Becca." He entered the courtroom and the door slowly closed behind him with a muted thud.

Becca sighed and went down the hall to the ladies' room to clear her head and then came back out and stopped once more in front of Courtroom A-3. She peeked inside through the smoked-glass panel.

The interior dimmed in the low light, and she couldn't hear a word even by pressing her ear to the glass. Her feet ached, the left one in particular. She lifted her foot out of the shoe. A circle of raw pink skin had blistered her heel. *Great. On top of everything else.*

The guard who monitored the hallway earlier had stepped away from his post. Two suits talking in hushed tones occupied the area where he once stood. She chewed on her fingernail and mulled the situation. She could do one of two things. Making a quick decision, she opened the door and went inside.

Chapter Seventeen

Becca's heartbeat thrummed like a blender set to puree. She hid in the shadows at the back of the courtroom where several rows of blue cushioned chairs lent the intimate feel of a small theater. Athena and Lark, along with her caseworker, Darrell Harding, sat together on one side of the aisle while Tony and the other lawyer sat on the other. Everyone's back was to her. She feared being spotted, but unless she coughed or sneezed, there would be little chance of attracting anyone's notice. The judge, the only one who faced in her direction, buried his nose in his paperwork and then perfunctorily addressed them as though he were already bored with the matter.

Becca's gaze riveted on Lark. Even in prison garb and close-cropped hair, she held a certain beauty. She cast her gaze to Darnell Harding and tried to pick up on something that might incriminate him. A look, a glance. Margie's voice floated in her head: *Looks like they were together...standing next to each other.* She didn't want to believe it. The words pierced her sensibilities. For her son's sake, she didn't want to believe her daughter-in-law capable of such betrayal.

The moment Tony got up to address the judge, Becca's heart leaped to her throat. Like a wound coil, her insides tightened with anticipation. She struggled to hear what he said and could make out just about everything with the exception of an occasional muted syllable that she filled in herself. He was on her side, and she hung on his every word, practically willing the proper inflection, tempo, pace, and timing would land agreeably on the judge's ear. It would have been perfect to have her friends testify on her behalf, but she was grateful for Tony's contribution. He had the experience the others didn't. She listened as he made their case...the mention of her and Paul's *hearts,* and how much Tally had adapted seamlessly to her environment. He even highlighted the little garden she tended at the supervision of Miss Bea. *Good work, Tony.*

Still uncomfortable at sneaking into the courtroom, she thought it best to leave now before someone came in and found her, particularly someone from Youth Services, and asked why she was there—a sure way to get unwanted attention. Now that Tony had made her case, there was nothing more she could do. The outcome of the judge's decision was out of her control. She moved toward the exit.

As Becca walked back up the aisle, she turned around for one last look. She focused on the judge, but she couldn't get a read on him; his stoic face appeared emotionless as though his features were etched in stone. Before she pulled open the door, the other lawyer stood and took the floor. He spoke and then addressed the judge. The next voice she heard was Lark's.

Becca stopped short. She strained at her daughter-in-law's words. Lark's barely audible voice all but disappeared into the room like vapor, except for the few words Becca was able to audibly discern: *Faithful. Family. Love.*

Becca's ire rose. She flushed in anger. *Faithful? Bull.* Becca let go of the door handle and listened in disbelief. Something pulled inside her; a force welled up. For a second, she fought her own will, but the inferno of rage could not be held in check. She turned back and stepped into the aisle.

"Excuse me." Her strident voice pierced the room. As soon as the words left her mouth, her knees buckled. The volcanic lava had exploded, and there was no way to put it back into the mountain, yet something inside welled and buoyed her courage to continue.

All heads turned in her direction. With the weight of their stares, a sense of empowerment came over her like never before.

Inflated with this power, she marched down the aisle with the intention of verbalizing the rest of her thoughts.

"No, Lark. I don't think so. I don't think you've been faithful at all—"

Judge Lazinsky banged his gavel and barked, "Ma'am, what is going on here and just who are you?"

Lark's expression fell, and she stared back at Becca as though she were an alien. Tony rushed across the room and up the aisle.

"Becca, what the Sam Hill are you doing?" The gruff edge in his voice bordered on anger. He took her by the arm back up the aisle.

Adrenaline surged in her veins. Becca pulled away. "No, Tony, you don't understand."

"What don't I understand?" His jaw dropped open and hung like a grouper fish.

"Judge," Becca began as she pushed past Tony. "I just want you to know there's more here than meets the eye."

"More than—first of all, you're out of line, Ms.—"

"I'm sorry, Judge," Tony interjected. "This is my client, Becca Wallace, Lark's mother-in-law."

The judge stared sternly. "Ms. Wallace, your being here is highly inappropriate. This is a closed hearing and—"

"We know, sir." Tony pressed his palms together and then held them up toward the judge. "If you will please excuse us just a moment."

Tony took Becca by the elbow and led her to the back of the room. "What's going on?" he demanded.

Becca pressed her fingers to her temples and shook her head. "I don't know."

"This isn't helping things, Becca."

She hated hearing people use her name as a punctuation mark.

"I know. I'm sorry. It's just that I needed to come in and hear what was going on." About to break down in tears, Becca fought her emotions. "I just couldn't bear to hear what she was saying."

"Lark?"

"Yes."

"Why?"

Becca shook her head. "Her lies."

"I'm not following."

"I couldn't believe what I was hearing." Becca frowned. *Faithfulness... family.* "She's full of it, Tony."

His eyes blinked in double time.

"Look, please listen to me. I have reason to believe that Lark's been unfaithful. I have proof. Physical proof."

"So, what are you telling me here, you're saying she has a lover?"

Becca lifted her blistered foot out of the tight leather, hoping to lessen the pain.

"Who is it, Becca?"

Becca paused before incriminating anyone. Though she was fairly certain Margie knew what she saw, the thought of placing immediate blame hit. Seconds later, she blurted out, "I'm pretty sure it's the caseworker, Darnell Harding."

Tony's face fell. He looked back toward the lawyer's table.

"Look, I don't know what to tell you at this point. I think the judge is just about through. I better go back down there." He patted her arm. "Go home, Becca." His voice softened. "I'll fill you in later on the next steps."

Becca stood stoic. She eased her sore foot back into her shoe and grimaced at the pain.

Chapter Eighteen

Margie came up to Becca the moment she entered the lobby. "Where'd you go?"

"Don't ask."

Margie's eyes widened. "You went in there, didn't you?"

Becca stood silent.

"You did!"

"I just couldn't stand another minute of waiting." She crossed her arms over her chest. "And her lies."

"What happened, Bec?" Jane held a hand to her throat as both women stared at her in disbelief, along with Pastor Benson.

"Did you testify?" Pastor Benson asked as he loosened his tie.

All three of them held puzzled looks of confusion. Becca gave a decisive nod and pointed to the front entrance.

"Let's go. I can't talk here. I'll explain outside." She took the lead and marched out the door.

Outside, they gathered around her by the corner of the courtyard where Becca laid out the whole extent of what happened in the courtroom.

"That galls me." Margie's words came out bitter. "Sorry, Bec."

"Me, too. So sorry, Becca," Jane echoed.

Pastor Benson pulled the handkerchief out of his breast pocket and mopped his brow.

Becca raked her hand along the back of her neck. "Yeah, if I could take it all back, I would. But my emotions just took over." She glanced inside the plate glass window at the front of the building and wondered if someone would be coming out to arrest her.

"Don't beat yourself up." Margie laid her hand on Becca's shoulder. "You did what you had to do."

“Took guts, honey,” Jane added.

“Becca, there’s not much I can say other than I feel your pain.” Pastor Benson’s face shone pink in the hot noonday sun. He placed his hand gently on her shoulder. “Why don’t we just pray now and see where this goes. Let’s just take it one minute at a time.”

After a short huddle, Pastor said the final amen and gave her a fatherly half-smile. “All is not lost, dear. Just wait on God. Don’t try to manipulate things.”

Becca nodded. She thanked everyone for their time and dismissed them with a wave as they departed for their cars. She understood his point. Though, inside, she remained torn. She couldn’t rock the boat too much, but deep down there was no way she would lose her granddaughter to an adulterer. No way at all. As embarrassing as her outburst was, she’d do it again and risk more than her pride to protect Tally.

Heat sizzled from the blacktop. Becca’s best silk blouse clung to her damp skin. She longed to peel it off. On the way to her car, she heard her name come from across the rows of cars. She glanced up. Her friend, Jane, waved at her from two rows over.

“Wait, I have something for you,” Jane called.

Becca signaled the okay sign and then clicked the door lock open. The front seat was oven-hot as she sat, and the backs of her thighs singed on the steaming leather. She quickly inserted the key into the ignition, flipped on the AC, and then hopped back out.

“I forgot to bring this the other day.” Jane plopped a box down on the macadam. “Just some of your stuff from your yard. Your lawn ornaments—the garden gnome, the pinwheel thingy, and—well, whatever I thought you’d want to keep.”

Becca’s heart melted with nostalgia as she peeked inside the flap. The ceramic bunny her dear neighbor Cyndy gave her before she moved away to Arizona sat among the collectables.

“Oh, that was too kind of you, Jane, thanks.”

Jane shrugged. "Nothing you wouldn't do for me."

Their friendship was equally reciprocal. She opened the passenger door and then picked up the box. As she placed it on the front seat, the cool air blasting from the AC vents blew on her forearm. The breeze lifted the top flap of the box and something shiny caught her eye. She reached inside and pulled it out.

"Hmmm, what's this?"

With an expression signaling she had no clue, Jane shrugged. "Oh, that. Yeah, I found it on your lawn right next to your house. In the flower bed. Looked pretty expensive."

The silver-plated lighter weighed heavy in the palm of her hand and shone like a mirror. Becca winced as the sun's rays reflected off the metal and bounced directly into her eyes. The initials *D. R. H.* were engraved on it.

Chapter Nineteen

Becca flicked the lighter open and watched the blue-orange glow as it lapped up the air. She shut the lid and tossed it into the box.

"Well," she said with a sigh, "thanks for you help...means a lot to me."

"No problem, sweetie. It'll all work out, you'll see."

Becca lent a feeble smile as a way of accepting her friend's attempt to prop up the situation.

"Now, call me, ya hear?" Jane held Becca by the shoulders. "Keep me abreast of your progress with this, okay? I'm here for you, honey."

"Thanks, I will," Becca replied.

Jane squeezed Becca's shoulders in a reassuring confirmation of the woman's loyalty. "Okay, then." She walked away and with a wave turned to say, "Don't forget to call, now."

Becca waved back. When she got into the car, she lowered the blasting AC to a softer breeze. Her initial doubts coalesced into one pure conclusion: the lighter could belong to only one person with the engraved initials *D. R. H.*

Her mind raced with possible scenarios of how Darnell Harding's fancy lighter ended up in the grass outside the charred remains of her old home. Did Lark sneak him into the house by way of the basement room at her mother and father-in-law's house when Jason was in prison and everyone else was asleep? Did someone leave it there to implicate him in the burning down of the house? Did he himself burn it down in anger at Lark over a quarrel? With each thought ringing potentially true, her anxiety level rose another notch.

The parking lot remained full, and cars overflowed onto the adjacent grass as she pulled around the back of the building, hoping for a fast way out. At the back entrance to the courthouse sat an unmarked white van. Beside it was the last person she imagined seeing: her daughter-in-law's caseworker, Darnell Harding.

Her heart seized as though danger were ahead. She didn't know what to do—say something? Keep moving? Or slow down and give him a scathing look? A quick decision led her foot abruptly to the brake pedal. She pressed hard and rolled down the window. He glanced her way and then did a double take.

"Mr. Harding," Becca began. "I'd like a word with you." Her heart thumped at her own boldness.

He stood tall in his suit. With his tie loosened, he mirrored a disheveled version of Denzel Washington. As he stepped forward, his face remained stoic.

"Ms. Wallace, we meet again."

Becca's insides squirmed. "Yes, Mr. Harding. Indeed, we do." She punctuated her words and turned off the engine before stepping out of the car. "Listen, sir. I'm not sure what's going on between my daughter-in-law and you but—"

"Going on?" He gave her a quizzical look.

"Yes, *going on*." She glanced over at the van and wondered if Lark was inside and chained up again for the ride back to prison. Her sentence was over in a few months, she figured. Though in keeping both her son's and daughter-in-law's criminal records straight with all of the shifting bureaucratic rules, she wasn't sure of Lark's exact date of release.

Darnell Harding took a step back and pulled off his glasses. "I'm not sure what you're referring to."

Becca's blood boiled at his nonchalance. "Really, sir? How is it that I really want to believe you?" She paused for effect. "But I can't. There's more to your relationship with Lark Wallace than I care to embellish right here and now. So, let's just be clear that one of us may not have all of the facts."

He smiled efficiently. "I guess that would be you, Ms. Wallace."

Becca remembered the picture Margie told her about, the one Athena showed Margie. He'd been standing with his arm around her, according to Margie, whose words quietly rang in her head... *it looked like they were together.*

"What are you implying, Ms. Wallace?"

To accuse him of adultery would be serious. Becca paused, hesitant to answer. Once the words were out, there would be no taking them back. She chewed the inside of her bottom lip, deciding whether any further accusatory comments would be worth it. No one else was around. Dropping bombs in the middle of a vacant desert would profit nothing. They needed to explode where they could cause the most damage to the enemy.

"Why don't you"—her index finger stabbed the air— "tell me the truth, Darnell?"

"The truth?" He rubbed the back of his head.

"Yes," she shouted. "The truth about your feelings for my daughter-in-law."

"Feelings?" He cast a fake smile to the ground. "Ma'am, I don't know what you're trying to imply here—"

"I'm implying that you're trying to squeeze my son out of his own marriage," she said, flustered with his pushback. "That's what I'm talking about." She hated feigned innocence and wanted to slap him. "And that's what's probably holding up the adoption. My rights are being spat upon because you're just so dead-set on letting Lark have Tally, and you're breaking the rules just to please her."

"It's our job to keep the children with the parents," Ms. Wallace. "But our decision has little or nothing to do with our personal feelings."

"Please," she said, shaking her head. "Parents who are incarcerated have no business raising children. May God have mercy on you, sir. You're doing an injustice to the little girl. Has anyone asked Tally where she wants to live?" Becca's anger seethed.

"There's something unkosher going on here, and I think I smell the source."

"That's not true, Ms. Wallace."

"You expect me to believe you?" Her exasperation now bordered on near-contempt.

She'd been patient for so long with the County and all of the red tape tying up their case. There was nothing she could do to speed up the adoption process; though, in the courtroom, it looked like she was losing ground in the battle. Hopefully, the truth would come out sooner or later.

Between the long-winded phone calls, copious paperwork, and dealing with the frustration of living in limbo, Becca was beyond tired of it. With all of her own grief, she wondered for the sake of Tally how the sweet child was processing the lifestyle she'd been thrust into.

"You asked for the truth. You want the whole truth?" he retorted.

"Yes. I. Would," she barked.

"Well, I'd be happy to tell you, Ms. Wallace. Have a minute?"

"I do."

Chapter Twenty

Becca got back in the car and braced herself for what Darnell Harding would say. She turned the engine on and flipped the AC vents toward her perspiring face.

"It's kind of hot outside, Ms. Wallace," he said. "Mind if I come inside your car? It's a long story."

Becca paused. "Sure," she replied, flatly. She figured he deserved the benefit of the doubt and due process, but she was hesitant in lending him any slack. In place of it, she offered him the coolness of her car. At least, he wouldn't swelter in the sun.

He took off his suit jacket and folded it over his arm. Then he walked around to the passenger side of the car and slid into the seat.

"Ah, that's better." He glanced toward her. "Appreciate it." He whipped his glasses off and wiped them with a cloth retrieved from his pocket and then placed them back on. He adjusted himself and squarely faced her. "Now, if I have my dates right, I met Lark about this time last year. Probably a good twelve or maybe even thirteen months ago." He thought a moment. "Yes, it was around mid-July. I was driving back on I-81 from an all-day conference, looking for a place to grab a beer and a light dinner before driving back home." He wiped his brow with the eyeglass cloth. "I figured Scranton was as good a place as any, so I headed into the downtown business district and walked to the nearest decent-looking bar I could find."

****

July 12, 2017

The sun hung low in the sky in downtown Scranton as he approached the door of McNear's Bar on Thirty-third Avenue.

"Welcome to McNear's. What'll it be?"

"Whatever's on tap." Darnell reached over and plucked a nut out of the bowl and popped it into his mouth.

"You got it."

He took a few more nuts and downed them. As the bartender poured the rich amber liquid, Darnell reached into the pocket of his suit jacket and brought out his wallet and a pack of Winstons. He lit a cigarette, inhaled, and slowly blew out the smoke. The bartender placed the beer on a coaster and pushed it toward him. He took another drag and began to relax as his tension eased.

"Thanks." He nodded and laid a twenty-dollar bill next to the glass.

"Anything else, buddy?"

He lifted his glass. "I'm good—for the moment."

The bartender nodded. "Okay, we'll settle up later."

Darnell took a sip and then another drag of his cigarette.

A tall figure stood in a smoky haze at the other end of the bar. When the smoke cleared, something about the man's image transported Darnell back to 1991, the time he served in the Gulf War.

"Got a light?" came the voice.

Darnell glanced up and saw the man from the end of the bar now seated a barstool away. He twirled a cigarette in Darnell's direction.

"Oh, yeah, sure." He flicked open his lighter as the man tilted his cigarette into the flame.

"Thanks." The man leaned back, and a puff of smoke exited his lips.

Something triggered Darnell. There was a familiarity about this stranger. He knew this guy, but from where, he didn't know. Over the next few minutes, he stole glances in the man's direction.

Darnell lit a second cigarette and turned to the man. "Do I know you?"

The man's head swiveled toward Darnell. His piercing green eyes landed like a dart, and, without a word from the man, something registered.

"Hold up. I *do* know you." He paused and pointed at him. "Ice?" he said, curiously.

Coolly, the man picked up his cigarette, inhaled, and slowly blew out a puff of smoke.

"Is it you, Ice?" Anticipation rose in Darnell's gut.

The man continued to stare.

"It's me. *Darnell.* Darnell Harding." He paused. "Hardball."

The man's mouth slowly curled up in the corners, followed by a slow nod.

"It *is* you!" Darnell grinned broadly. He reached out and slapped the man on the back—his old army buddy, the one who once saved his life in the heat of an unexpected strike.

The man put down his cigarette, still keeping his focus on Darnell. In a slow-motion drawl, he said, "Well, I'll be a son-of-a-buck's hide if I ain't. Last time I saw you, you were knee deep in dirt and shrapnel."

Darnell could still hear the artillery mortar fire that nearly claimed his life as a young soldier, along with visions of flying debris from a roadside bomb that exploded less than one hundred feet from their position.

"There was no escape," he said, recalling the close call when two pieces of large shrapnel flew by his head and settled in the opposite side of the hole. "You know, if you hadn't jumped in front—well, let's just say the only reason I survived was because of you."

Ice gave a modest grin and downed his beer. "If you wanna say that, there's no stoppin' ya, but I ain't no one's hero, that's for sure."

"I'd have to beg to differ on that one," Darnell countered. "In fact, I've owed you ever since that day. You never cashed in."

The man gave a perfunctory half-grin and shrugged.

Darnell took a final drag on his cigarette, amazed at the serendipity of the moment and snuffed out the stub. Recalling the fateful incident that almost took his life, he remembered the vow he'd made to his combat buddy. Anything this man wanted that was in his power to do, he would do it. No questions asked. He pulled out one of his business cards and slid it across the bar toward the man's glass. "If you ever need me for anything."

The man palmed the card and stared. "Not too shabby. Like your work?"

"Can't say I don't." He shrugged. "Pays the bills." He paused. "So, what's been going on in your life these days...married?"

The man shook his head. "Nope, no one in my life right now." He raised his hand to signal the bartender and pushed his empty glass forward. He reached over and plucked out a couple of the larger nuts in the bowl. "But I'm good with it." He nodded. "Women." He shrugged. "Lotta sorrow and pain with that breed, know what I'm sayin'?"

The look in his eyes told Darnell a different story. He wore his loneliness like neon. He'd always worn a false front. Fearless. Daring. Bold. He appeared to have it all together in the face of danger, but Darnell remembered a different side of him.

Amid their recollections, an abrupt crash rocked the bar. Ice snapped his eyes shut and held the edge of the bar stool; his fingers pressed into the thick leather padding. The clatter came from the kitchen, and the bartender stopped what he was doing, threw down a rag, and headed for the swinging doors.

Moments later, Ice opened his eyes and took in the room. Darnell followed his gaze toward the stacked rows of beer and wine glasses on the wall-to-wall mirror hanging behind the bar. No one else seemed affected by the noise. The few patrons sitting in the dim interior remained absorbed in their food and conversation.

"Damn," he grunted under his breath.

"You okay?"

"Oh, sure."

At the other end of the bar, the bartender, mop in hand, stood at the kitchen entryway where, apparently, someone had dropped a tray of plates and glassware. It occurred to Darnell that Ice may have PTSD. What had just happened was not mortal gunfire but rather a clumsy bus boy's personal calamity.

"Just an accident in the kitchen," Darnell assuaged him.

Ice's right hand shook as he picked up the glass. After downing the drink, he teased out another cigarette. Darnell picked up his lighter and aimed the flame in the man's direction. He snapped the lid shut when a dark-haired woman approached and took a seat at the bar. Darnell couldn't help but admire her beauty and had seen her before, but it was Ice who let out a low whistle.

"Wow," he said under his breath. "Hot mama."

"Yes, she's a looker all right. But before you swing your bat, she's married."

He frowned. "How'd you know?"

"I know. And her story isn't pretty, so set your sights somewhere else, my friend."

"What? You know her?"

"Not the way you think, perhaps. But, yeah, I know her. Sort of. I've seen her at the prison and know her situation."

"She's been in the pen?"

He shrugged. "Might have. Nobody's business, right?"

The woman pulled out something from her purse and laid it on the table in front of the bartender.

"Must have gotten carded," Ice said under his breath. "How old is she?"

"Don't know, but I'm sure she's of age." He chuckled. "I think the bartender just wanted to know her name. Have a cousin who was still carded at thirty-nine. Some people just have that look, ya know?"

The woman sipped her drink and stared ahead as though stuck in her thoughts. The bartender hovered in her space, wiping down glasses and setting them on a white cloth. They eventually struck up a conversation, and before long, Darnell heard her say the word, *ride.* Apparently, she needed a lift somewhere and mentioned *Chester County* and *bus* in the same sentence. Ice kept his eye on her and then collected his change lying by the empty glass. As they continued making small talk, Ice signaled her attention with his hand.

"Ma'am," he called to her. "You need a ride somewhere?"

Her eyebrows lifted. "Um, well, yeah, but there's a bus." She raised her thumb and gestured behind her.

"Where to?"

"Where am I going?"

"Yeah."

"Chester County."

Ice snuffed out the remaining butt of his cigarette and stood. He glanced at himself in the mirror and then swept his hair from his eyes. "I'm headed that way...going right through there. Live in Delaware County. If you need a lift, my truck's right around the corner."

The woman gave a modest smile. "Are you sure—I mean, I hate to put you out or anything."

"No problem at all. It's time I got home anyway. Been working on a job up here for three straight weeks. Could use some down time."

"What do you do?" She removed her sunglasses from atop her head and picked up the napkin sitting under her glass.

"Contracting—roofs, clean-up, masonry. Do it all," he replied as she absently wiped her sunglasses with the napkin while keeping her gaze on him. "Whatever needs doing." He gestured toward the door. "You need to go now, or—?"

"Sure, anytime, really. Now is fine." She adjusted the strap of her purse and rolled off the barstool.

"Okay, be back in a second." Ice pointed his thumb to the restroom.

Darnell glanced at his watch and mentally assessed how long it would take to get back home to Philadelphia. He settled with the bartender and took one more handful of nuts before leaving. The young woman glanced at him and gave a knowing look as he neared.

"Hey," she said, a coyness in her tone.

Darnell smiled. He briefly knew of her situation. To have a small child and a co-dependent drug and alcohol partner under one roof would be tough on any family. Having a daughter himself, Darnell's heart went out to her.

"I remember you." She smiled sweetly. "From Youth Services."

Darnell nodded. "Nice to see you again."

"Same here," she said, demurely.

Ice came up behind them.

Darnell turned to him. "And you, buddy...it was great running into you again. God bless you." Darnell gave Ice a casual salute and then patted him on the shoulder. "Remember"—he pointed his index finger to the man's chest—"I owe you."

Ice straightened his shoulders and said, with a slight curve in his lips, "If you say so."

Darnell grinned. "You bet'cha." He watched his old pal and Lark walk to the door and followed right behind them out to the street.

****

Becca let his words settle as the story took shape in her mind. She continued to focus on Darnell's body language. She knew the signs of a liar, the incessant blinking and swallowing that gave them away, but with Darnell she didn't notice anything even remotely not right about his story.

"Yes, but what about the picture?"

Darnell's face contorted. "What picture?"

"The one of you and Lark. Apparently, it was taken at some point when you were with her. I'm only assuming—"

"I don't recall taking a picture with her, Ms. Wallace." His eyebrows crinkled underneath the thick black frames of his glasses.

"Someone I know saw a picture of you," she said, measuredly. "My source says it was you. Definitely you."

"Me? You sure?"

"Do pictures lie?" she said, smartly.

"No, no they don't. But wait now..." He pointed his finger in the air and shook it for emphasis. "You know, I guess maybe there was a picture," he said. "I vaguely recall a flash just as we came to the front door of her home. A woman was taking pictures, and I came in to use the facilities. It was a long ride."

"So, you got caught in the picture, is that what you're saying?"

He raised his eyebrows. "Well, it was a long time ago but yup, guess I did." He gave a smug grin. "What can I say?"

"So, how did you come to be at her house if this old pal of yours, this Ice person, left with her?"

"Okay, yes, I'll tell you," he replied matter-of-factly. "There's a simple explanation for that."

Becca nodded and thought, *okay, let's hear it*. She wanted to say, *I'm waiting*, but thought better than to act superior at a time like this. She took the high road and without a word waited for his explanation. If this were a trap that he'd dug for himself, his own words would incriminate him at some point. With a hidden smugness, she waited for his reply.

"Well, the story with my buddy, Ice, is that as it turned out, he wasn't able to drive Lark home after all."

"How's that?"

"Unfortunately, his truck had broken down."

How convenient.

"Since I was heading for Philadelphia myself, stopping in Chester County was no problem... right on my way."

"So that's it? That's the whole story?" She thought his smooth talking may have been a bit too smooth.

"That's it," Darnell replied. He raised his eyebrows and both hands in surrender mode. "I'm sorry to disappoint you, Ms. Wallace, but I have never had an interest in your daughter-in-law, except for a platonic one."

His story sounded honest enough, innocuous even. Though as Becca studied him further, there was something about his vibe that didn't quite square. Were things as neat and tidy as he presented them? Or was there more information left unsaid? Although she believed his story—even the last detail about taking Lark directly home from the bar in Scranton— something didn't thrum. A lingering doubt hovered as though there were a few missing pieces from the puzzle.

Rather than push the situation, she swallowed her curiosity and stifled the urge for more information. Potentially, there was a chance she might need further help from him someday; now was not the time for burning any bridges. Pressing him beyond his comfort level would take a back seat—for now.

As the picture came into a clearer focus, at least, from the perspective he'd shared, Becca wanted more. Also, she wanted to communicate with Lark one-on-one about the matter and longed to confirm her suspicions. Today wouldn't be the best time as it was already well past noon, but there was always tomorrow.

"Okay," she said as graciously as possible. "Thanks for the information."

Darnell lifted the door handle and nodded. "My pleasure, Ms. Wallace. Glad we could straighten things out." He opened the car door and left.

Chapter Twenty-One

All night, Becca slept restlessly. Anxious thoughts swirled through her dreams. Her plans to adopt Tally proved more daunting than she thought. But she would reach the bottom of this one way or another and wanted nothing more than clear evidence for the authorities, so they could reach their own conclusions on who would be the best custodians for Tally. She would leave nothing up for grabs about the case, and she'd fight, making certain in the final determination that she and Paul would get the child, because they were the only potentially fit people to raise her.

The following morning, Becca got up early and set the kitchen table for Tally and Paul's breakfast. She filled bowls of granola, poured apple juice, and placed two slices of gluten-free raisin bread into the toaster. She took out the butter and placed it on the table along with Tally's vitamins and Paul's pills. Miss Bea would be coming soon to take care of Tally for the day after Paul left for work, and she was grateful to have the kind neighbor's support.

From the night before when Becca pointed out the necessity for meeting with Lark, Paul knew her plans for the day and where she was going. He warned her to be careful and not read too much into Lark's comments, knowing that they could be a smokescreen for the truth. He instructed her to take Lark's end of the conversation with a grain of salt, believing drug addicts not only fool themselves but others as well.

"Paul, I'm leaving now. Breakfast is all ready," she called into the bedroom. "Miss Bea should be here any minute."

He came down the hall. "Okay, drive carefully," he instructed.

"I will."

They hugged and he planted a kiss on her forehead before she grabbed her purse and opened the door.

"Be safe."

"I will," she called back to him as the door closed.

****

Becca first filled up the gas tank and then took the back roads to the Northeast extension of the turnpike. Traffic moved along well and remained up-to-speed until there was a slowdown for construction with lane restrictions approaching Lansdale. She crawled for about a mile or so in the bumper-to-bumper traffic before the roadway opened up and turned back into a clear sail.

After a couple of hours, a stretch of blue-gray mountains rose in the distance. She knew Scranton wasn't far at this point, and she began to recall her childhood days and visits with relatives in the old coal mining town. Once a booming industrial area, the city's skyline, set against the serenity of the blue ridges of the Pocono Mountains, reminded her of faded actresses past their prime, struggling to remain relevant. The small blue-collar town didn't outwardly have much going for it now, and during its economic downturn held some of the highest incarceration rates in Pennsylvania.

Her mood sobered at thinking her only son and his wife made their part-time residence at a prison in the likes of six-by-eight-foot cells of rock and metal rather than a typical, quiet ranch-style home in the rolling hills and dales of the Pocono Mountains.

Becca got off at the Scranton exit and meandered through the historic business district containing late Victorians and Classical Revival designed structures. She followed the Mapquest directions and pulled up to the Lackawana prison. Luckily, there was a parking spot not far from the entrance on the street. *Ok, this is a good start.*

The façade of the yellowed bricks architecturally resembled a miniature castle. With its prominent towers, the structure must have been built sometime in the 1800s. She checked her purse to make sure she had her ID and took off her rings and gold chain bracelet, knowing jewelry wasn't allowed past a certain point. She peered at her face in the rearview mirror and reapplied her lipstick before stepping out.

Becca walked up the sidewalk to the front entrance and waited to be checked in. The attendant greeted her, and after a thorough vetting through a pat-down and the typical prison protocols, she waited anxiously by the door leading to the cell blocks.

Beyond the door, faint sounds of guards barking their orders seeped in along with shrill screams. A sense of desperation hung in the air. Becca bristled at the austerity. The vent directly above her channeled air just shy of being cool enough to do much good. To distract herself, she counted the squares in the linoleum floor—maroon, white, maroon, black. After counting to one hundred, she started over.

The course of her daughter-in-law's history since she became part of the family was one continuous cycling in and out of prison for petty drug sales. Becca bore guilt for Lark's prison stays. She heaped an emotional burden on herself because she believed Jason was the one who got Lark involved in the sordid lifestyle of drugs. He'd been a decent kid for most of his life but turned for the worst not long after Becca took him away from his father and ran to a safe house. It was the best course of action after Rob's threats had stolen the better of her. But she'd never go back to that man and would rather die than live with him and subject her son to that lifestyle. Though, now, she believed the toll for leaving him was coming back to bite her.

"This way," the guard said, waving her on. Becca got up and followed him down a narrow hall leading into a large room. Humid air saturated the entire prison; even the cells and hallways were kept captive by the close air. A man in a suit stood talking with a woman in street clothes, along with a female inmate, on the far side of the room. A few tables and chairs were scattered throughout, and a row of cushioned folding chairs lined one of the walls.

Becca had too much energy to sit. For now, she just stood in place by the first row of chairs. Not long afterward, a buzzer rang as the door opened, and Lark appeared, accompanied by one of the guards.

Becca's heart dropped at the sight of her daughter-in-law in the hideous orange jumpsuit. Seeing Lark at the courthouse with her formerly long, wavy hair cropped into a boyishly short style, Becca was surprised. But now she was shocked at seeing the curves of Lark's slender body—a few pounds short of a skeleton—practically disappear in the oversized clothing.

"Hi, how are you Lark?" Becca kept her voice light and airy in an effort to break the ice between them. Her anger simmered just below the surface as she lent a pretend smile.

"Hey," Lark replied, not revealing any sign of emotion. She leaned in and wrapped her arms loosely around her mother-in-law, and Becca responded in kind.

It was one thing to mentally prepare for an altercation, but in the frisson of the here and now as she held her ground and stood face-to-face with the girl, something inside gave her pause. Becca held a restraint on her emotions as though she wore a bit and bridle to keep her tongue under control. During the two-hour drive to the prison, she'd rehearsed what she planned to say. Even during the one-sided narrative, her emotions grew hot. Now that the opportunity was here, she would keep things measured and even, lest her anger boil over and lead to a fight.

"You must be surprised to see me," Becca said as she pulled out of the stiff embrace.

Lark shrugged and lent a ghost of a smile, her eyes sheepish.

"This shouldn't take long." Becca gestured to the row of cushioned folding chairs that occupied the large room and sat down. In a silent command, she patted the chair beside her.

Lark slid into the seat next to Becca and stared at her lap before lifting her eyes and saying, "Are you mad at me for something? At the hearing, you seemed upset. I'm not sure what that was about. I guess that's what you want to talk about?"

"Yes, I'd like to discuss a few things with you." Becca's tone turned firm. Her words defied the gnawing fear inside. She put on a bold front and continued. "First of all, I want to know something. About Jason."

"Jason?" Lark's voice softened. "What about Jason?"

"I want to know how you feel about him. Do you love him?"

Lark's expression turned curious. "Becca," she began. Her brows knit. "Where's this coming from? I mean, why would you—"

"I want to know the truth, young lady." Becca's words sliced over Lark's. Her heart raced.

"Look, I'm in prison. I miss my husband—not to mention my baby girl, terribly. How are they doing?" Lark's green eyes turned doleful.

"Tally is doing well. Very well." Becca nodded.

"How's Jason? Is he out of the hospital yet?"

"No, he's still there." She glanced down at her shoes and was glad she wore the comfortable flats today. She could use all the comfort she could get. "He's still in physical therapy. Seems to be doing much better now. He should be released in a couple of weeks."

"I'm so glad to hear you tell me that. I've been worried about him. And depressed. I hate it here, and I just want to be back home—with all of you."

Becca held firm as her emotions swayed. *Of course, you want to come back home. Home is where you're free to do what you want and with whom. Maybe even burn down another house. But it won't be ours.* She hated herself for thinking this way and tried to push the dark thoughts out. *Stay the course, Becca. Just tell her what's on your mind.*

"So, let me ask you again." Becca began. "Do you love my son?"

"Yes," she said, her voice rising. "Of course, I do!"

Becca tried to read her body language. Earlier, she prayed her words wouldn't come out rancorous like at the hearing when she lost her cool. Now, face-to-face with Lark, and in the presence of those watching possibly through hidden cameras, her tone bordered on the precarious edge between civility and hostility. She thought better to dial it back. She needed to remain measured, or the meeting with Lark would be over. Becca braced herself and took a deep breath.

"Lark, I'm sorry to have to bring this up. It's been on my mind, and I might be off base, but it's just a feeling." She lowered her gaze to the floor in an effort to gather her courage. "And I understand circumstantial evidence sometimes looks bad, I know." She raised her eyes to meet her daughter-in-law's, fearful of what she was wading into. "But I have reason to believe that you have something going on...with—"

"With who?"

"With a person—"

"Who?" Lark shook her head. "I'm not following you."

"You—and...someone—"

"With another *man*?" Lark's face crinkled. "Is that what you're trying to say?"

"Yes, Lark. Yes, that's exactly what I'm saying," Becca said, evenly. She focused her eyes on Lark. She had hoped things would not escalate and that the truth would come out. The tension in her stomach kicked up a notch, now defying her earlier semi-confidence. Paul's words repeated in her head... *Are they still together? Drugs are a strange mistress.* In the strained silence, the air sizzled.

"Becca, look. I've sold drugs and dabbled in them a few times. I got caught and now I'm paying the price. Sorry to be such a disappointment to you, but it doesn't mean I'm a bad person"—she lowered her head— "or am leaving Jason because he got me into this mess." She raised her head boldly as though bravely confronting the next blow. "And, no, I am not involved with anyone. I love my family—both Jason and Tally." She paused. "So, he's okay? He's healing from the accident?" she asked, her tone less strident.

"Like I said, he's getting better every day."

"That's so good to hear."

"I'm sure it is."

"Not much help I can be here, locked up." Lark cast her gaze around the room. "I feel so useless."

Becca struggled with what to say. There could have been several things she could have laid on her, chief of which was: *You reap what you sow*. She swallowed the pithy cliché and managed a neutral reply. "Well, the bright side is you won't be here forever," she offered, dispassionately. "If your record stays clean in here, it'll carry a lot of weight when your parole comes near."

Lark gave a short nod, appearing to understand. The optic white light from the overhead fluorescent strip bounced from floor to ceiling and highlighted the dark circles under her eyes. Even in the unforgiving light, her beauty still held a candle over most everyone else.

Becca cast her gaze around the room. Stains marked the ceiling similar to the ones in her old bedroom on the third floor of her parents' Victorian—the curve of the rust-colored leak resembled the coast of South America. Becca had longed for a new coat of paint but never got it before she eloped.

"So, there's nothing between you and Darnell Harding?" Becca asked, pointedly, not letting go of the subject.

Lark squinted her eyes. "Darnell? Darnell is my caseworker. Or used to be until he got promoted. I don't know, maybe he still is. I can't keep all of the names straight." She shook her head questioningly. "Why would you bring up Darnell?"

"I saw a picture...a picture of you and him together."

"A picture?"

"Actually, I didn't see it myself, but a friend of mine did, and she said it looked...well, incriminating."

"A picture of me and Darnell Harding?"

Becca bit the inside of her cheek and lent a curt nod.

"I can't even...I'm not sure when or even why—oh, okay, yes," she said. "I remember now. Darnell drove me home one time after visiting Jason. I was staying at Mom's for the weekend—with Tally. The woman loved taking pictures with her new phone and started snapping away the minute I came through the door. Darnell came in with me to use the bathroom."

Becca wanted to believe Lark. She sensed her daughter-in-law's testimony was real. Those were the exact words Darnell had told her in his story. *Of course, Lark loved her family. How could I be so stupid?* The story rang true. Becca's insides slowly eased. The edges of her hard feelings toward the girl waned like softened wax.

As it neared the end of the allotted visiting time, Lark and Becca's encounter solidified as best as it could, considering the circumstances of their limited engagement and Lark's separation from the family. Becca hoped Lark's sentence would be coming to an end soon or that she could be let off for good behavior. If it was meant that she and Jason could become a real family, it would be the happiest day of Becca's life and an answer to prayer. She kept her hopes alive.

"The guard just signaled that we have five minutes left," Lark said under her breath.

"That was fast." Becca made a face at the evaporated time.

"Um... I just want to tell you one more thing." Lark ran her hand down the back of her head, smoothed her close-cropped hair a few times, and then grabbed the back of her neck with both hands. "Oh, I don't know how to say this."

"Yes?"

"I just want you to know—well, it meant nothing to me, really. But I did meet a guy— accidentally, I must say."

"Oh?"

"Yeah," Lark replied, sounding disappointed.

"What happened?" Becca braced for the worst.

"Well, you know, it started out so innocently. I mean, this guy...I met him up near the prison. I wanted to take Tally that day, but you said it would be best to keep her home, remember?"

Becca's mind raced to when this could have occurred, but off the top of her head, she couldn't remember and not wanting to interrupt, kept listening.

"Anyway, Chevon drove me there but she couldn't stay—I forget why...something about needing to get to somewhere. So, I figured I'd take a bus back home. I stopped at a bar to ask about the bus route. Turned out I must have dropped my license when the bartender carded me, and this guy in the bar found it and tracked me down. Came to the house and everything."

Becca bit the inside of her cheek in anticipation of what was coming. *Please don't tell me you slept with him.*

"It was so strange, like he was really trying too hard, or something." She crossed her arms over her stomach and eyed the guard. "I thanked him profusely for returning my license, but I wondered, why didn't he just mail it? Anyway, I'm not even sure how he found me since my license had the old address."

"So, what about this guy?" Becca interrupted "Did he make advances, or—?"

"Oh, well, yeah. I told him I was married and even introduced him to Tally, who was playing with her friends. You know, just to let him know that I wasn't interested, but he just hung around staring at me."

"Hmmm, odd."

"I guess. But then when Tally fell from the swing, he was right there for us...so helpful. Even wanted to take her to the ER."

"Wait. She fell?" Becca's chest tightened.

"Oh, she was okay and all. I was scared. I thought she broke something, but she was fine."

"You never told me," Becca shot back.

Lark bit her lip. "I didn't want to worry you. Besides, she didn't break anything." She swatted the air as though dismissing the incident. "It was just scary is all."

"When was this?"

Lark shook her head. "*Pffft,* I don't remember—awhile back." She waved her hand. "Last summer sometime."

Becca wondered how many other incidents had happened to the child without her knowledge. *All the more reason to get custody.*

"Then I ran into him at the mall. He was with a blonde-haired woman. He was really nice and chatted me up. Introduced me to the lady and all. Then, when I was ready to leave—Tally was getting antsy and pulling my arm—he kept talking like we were old friends." Lark rolled her eyes.

"Well, I'm glad you explained things and didn't—"

"Time!" announced the guard in a loud, buffoonish voice. He walked toward Lark, who gave him a rueful expression.

Already? Becca couldn't believe the visitation was over.

Lark's face folded as though defeated.

"But I thought..." Becca's words faded as the guard came forward. She quickly held open her arms to give Lark a final hug before he whisked her back to her holding cell.

Chapter Twenty-Two

On the turnpike traveling home from Scranton, Becca fiddled with the radio and tried to find a clear signal. Her spirits lifted since talking with Lark, and she couldn't wait to tell Paul about her experience at the prison. The misconception on her part now ironed out and the burden off her chest, she was grateful she had made the effort to talk with Lark one-on-one. Not that she didn't believe Darnell Harding was telling the truth. In her heart, she sensed his innocence and that he was being truthful, but she needed to hear it from Lark.

Unfortunately, even with her daughter-in-law's chaste behavior, Lark's lack of restraint when it came to drugs was an altogether other problem. It tore at Becca that Lark and Jason were not living their best lives all because of the poor choices they'd made. She silently prayed as she'd done numerous times: *God, please intervene in the situation.*

Becca eventually found a clear signal amid all the static just as a traffic report came on. The reporter rattled off the main road conditions in Philadelphia and then segued to information about the suburban roads. She kept an ear tuned for any mention of the Pennsylvania Turnpike. Moments later, the reporter announced there were no reported problems, except for sun glare slowing things down in the westbound direction from Norristown through Valley Forge. Later, when she exited the Northeast Extension and merged onto the turnpike at the Norristown interchange, the traffic was heavy but moving just as the reporter mentioned. By her calculations, she'd be home in another hour, hopefully, sooner.

Less than a mile from home, Becca stopped at the grocery store for a few staples and, while standing in line at the checkout, grabbed a bottled water and drank it on the spot. On the way back to the car, she lingered at the summer sidewalk sale displays offered by the adjacent strip mall.

The young girl who stood by the clothing racks and tables of merchandise cluttering the narrow walkway took Becca back to the summer she was seventeen when she had worked for a retail store at an outdoor mall. A friend, who managed the store, asked her to help during the Memorial Day holiday weekend. She could never figure out why they brought all of the stock outside only to parade it in the bright sunlight. Were they so hard up that they had to make a desperate plea for a potential buyer? Would the merchandize carry more appeal being nearer to the parking lot?

Now, as Becca juggled the grocery bags, she quickly browsed the table displays and inspected the assorted merchandise baking in the hot afternoon sun. Along the way, she spotted something from the arts and crafts store—a craft kit that looked interesting for Tally. It was half-price, so she bought it.

****

Becca pulled up to the apartment. Her back ached from the long drive, and she mentally tallied the seconds until she could get out of her shoes. Even the flats caused her pain after a while. She gathered the bags from the back seat and headed inside.

She stepped into the stuffy front hallway, close with humidity, and rang the doorbell. She braced for one of Tally's hugs, the child being the one bright spot in her life next to Paul. Like a spritely pet, as soon as she heard the doorbell, Tally always ran to greet whomever was behind the door. Becca waited patiently, despite her aching feet. *Come on, someone please open the door.*

The hall remained unusually quiet. Not even the familiar footsteps of the upstairs neighbor, Mr. Porter, could be heard.

His clomping had become a fixture by now. At first, the chronic thumping noise bothered her, but after meeting the poor soul, her heart softened. The sounds of his walking indicated he was getting around on his own. He was trying to lose weight, and his movement was a good thing. Today, maybe he had enough gumption to go to the park or jogging trail.

Becca rang the bell again. No answer. She figured they were probably out back on the patio. Paul had set up a little wading pool for Tally earlier in the season, and she loved it. As Becca stood in the humid hall, her face flushed. No wonder they were outside on a day like today. Becca put the parcels down and fumbled for the door key.

"I'm home," she called breezily through the half-open door. "Anyone home?" She carried the bags inside, quickly kicked off her shoes, and tossed her handbag and keys onto the hall table. "Hello?"

Silence filled the apartment, and the patio door was closed and locked. She peeked outside through the slats in the vertical blinds. The empty wading pool on the patio glistened like a turquoise jewel in the late afternoon sun. She went into Tally's room and found the bed made and nothing out of place, except for two things: Her favorite doll, Beatrice, wasn't on the bed as usual, and the top bureau drawer hung half-open.

Becca hastened out of the apartment and went around back. Were Tally and Miss Bea somewhere on the grounds, either taking a walk or feeding the ducks? Barefoot, she jogged down the walkway toward the courtyard. Not a soul in sight. She jogged farther down toward the swimming pool, where a few of the older residents sat together in the shade, and then hastened up toward the edge of the property. There was no one at the pond except the ducks. The concern she had bordered on worry now. Her stomach cinched. She came back and circled around the apartment building the same way she had entered five minutes earlier. There was no sign of either of them.

Chapter Twenty-Three

Earlier the same day

At twelve-thirty, Margie finished the last of her ham and cheese sandwich. She got up, brushed the crumbs from her palms, and knocked on her boss's door. "Pastor?" Margie said through the crack. "Excuse me...hope I'm not interrupting."

He glanced up from his desk. "No, no, come in. What's on your mind, Margie?"

"Your afternoon trip to the hospital today...I was wondering if I can go with you?"

He glanced down and held a finger to his desk calendar. "Let's see here."

"Your visit with the sick and shut-ins," she offered. "Is it okay? I'm pretty much caught up, and I've got most of the gift baskets organized. I'm just waiting for the printout of all the new home buyers in the area to arrive."

"Don't see why not."

"Great."

He checked his watch. "Okay, then. Let me check out the facilities, and I'll meet you at my car in five."

"Sounds good. Thank you, sir."

****

Margie and Pastor approached the visitor's desk of Holy Cross Hospital and signed in. The lady behind the desk handed over the requisite name badges.

"Pastor, I confess, I wanted to come here today for a reason." She pulled the tape off and placed the nametag on her chest.

"Oh?" He raised his eyebrows.

"Yes. Well, you know the newborn I found back in April? I just wanted to stop by to see how he—or she—is doing." She smiled. "I've thought of little else since then."

"Of course, Margie." He turned back to the lady at the information desk. "Excuse me, but we're looking for a baby."

Margie chuckled to herself at the way he phrased the request. She stepped closer to the desk and interjected, "I found a baby a few months ago and turned it into—rather, took the infant to the emergency room. Can you let us know how the baby is doing?"

The elderly woman paused and held two fingers to her lips as she processed the question. "Um, I'm pretty sure we don't keep the babies here. At least not for long. I can check, but I'm fairly certain that once they're examined by the doctor and they're given a clean bill of health, the babies are sent out for adoption."

"Could you tell us which agency?" Margie asked.

The woman pointed toward the hallway. "First door on your left down this hall. They should have all the information you need."

"Great, thanks," Margie said. "Pastor, how about I check it out and meet up with you?" She pointed behind her in the direction of the hall. "Oh, wait. Whose room did you plan to visit first?"

"Well, let's see." He pulled out his portable leather Day-Timer.

Her boss, ever the traditionalist. The whole world owned cell phones where their appointments could be stored, but Lou Benson preferred to hold on to the twentieth century with his notepaper and Parker pen.

"I'd like to start on the fourth floor. Evelyn Fielding should be there, and if time permits, we'll visit Barbara Rumson."

"Were you planning on seeing Jason? Jason Wallace?"

"Oh, my, of course. If he's still here. I've been meaning to catch up with him since his accident. Yes, let's see him first." He leaned over the desk. "Excuse me, is Jason Wallace still here at the hospital?"

The woman typed the name into the computer. "Hmmm. Okay, looks like he's over in the step-down unit. Room 418." She pointed to the left. "Elevator is down the first hallway. Go through the lobby and make a left just past the gift shop."

Pastor Benson raised his hand. "Thank you."

"I feel so sorry for him," Margie said as they walked to the elevator.

Pastor smoothed down his name badge. "I know."

"The family has been through so much."

Pastor Benson clutched his Bible to his chest and nodded as they boarded.

"The Lord must be refining them," she added.

"True, indeed. Some by the fire...some through the flood." He pushed the button for the fourth floor.

Margie recognized the words to the old hymn and began to hum it in her head as the elevator ascended. It was then that Margie realized she'd forgotten to stop and check with the people about the baby. She made a mental note to do it after the visitation.

At the fourth floor, they stepped out. She said a silent prayer for Jason and his family as, shoulder to shoulder, she and the pastor walked together down the corridor.

"This is it, Pastor." She pointed to the wall plaque at the doorway that read *418*."

He stopped short, turned, and she followed behind him as he entered the room.

Margie never liked invading people's space, especially when they were in bed, but this was different. Jason wasn't sick or indigent. He'd just fallen on bad times. Something inside her ached to help him, if only to hold his hand and let him know she cared.

Jason lay staring at the wall-mounted TV, holding the remote as they entered.

"Jason!" Pastor Benson greeted in an upbeat tone as he neared the bed. "How's it going, son?"

The patient shrugged. "Think I'll live."

"Indeed, you will. Hope you're doing better these days. You've been on our minds and hearts big-time." The pastor patted Jason's shoulder.

"So sorry to hear of your accident, Jason," Margie said. "I've been praying for you."

"I need all the prayers I can get," Jason said, flatly.

She held his gaze. "You doing okay?"

"I'm good."

Jason's doleful eyes melted her heart. The look took her back to when she was his Sunday School teacher so many years ago. He'd said the same thing with the exact expression after one of the kids picked on him. Disappointment was etched all over his face, but at her attempt to console him, he'd replied that he was *okay.* She sensed then, much the same as now, that he might be hiding the truth.

Pastor Benson placed his Bible on the nearby chair. "Considering everything, you've come a long way." He clasped his hands together. "You're on the mend, son."

Margie moved across the room and sat by the window while pastor chatted with Jason.

"Listen, I wanted to share something with you." Pastor Benson picked up the Bible and began flipping through the pages. He frowned. "Now, where is it?" Rifling through the loose paper sandwiched inside the back flap, he shook his head. "Well, looks like I left it on my desk." He playfully slapped the side of his head.

"The story about the fire?" Margie asked, softening the word *fire* to a rough whisper.

Pastor shook his head. "No, no. Something else. Anyway, it was something I wanted to read to you." Pastor removed his suit jacket. "Maybe it's in here." He checked the inside pockets. "I thought it would be encouraging to hear how this young man, not much older than you, cleaned himself up—you, know, how he turned his life around," he amended. "Very inspiring."

Jason's eyes turned glassy under the harsh blue-white light. His gaze shifted to somewhere out the window as he blinked back tears. His body language gave himself away that he was troubled by something. Margie knew whatever it was weighing the boy down must have been deep. She had seen the expression before. Her heart melted for him.

"Is there something—" Pastor began.

"I didn't start any *fire*," Jason said, abruptly. "I'd never hurt my mother or Paul. Ever."

Margie startled at the abrupt outburst. A pang of regret hit. He must have heard her say the word *fire*.

"For what it's worth, I don't believe for a moment you had anything to do with the fire," Pastor said in an assuring tone. "I know you wouldn't do such a thing. It wasn't an accusation—"

"She didn't deserve it," he cried, as his words sliced over the pastor's. He buried his head in his pillow. Then, the words, "I had to do it," came out muffled. At least, that's what Margie thought she heard.

"Talk to me, son," Pastor Benson pleaded. "I'm here for you. *What* did you have to do?"

Chapter Twenty-Four

Jason lay motionless on the bed staring at the ceiling. His silence spoke loudly that he wasn't ready to talk, or he was having an inner battle with himself. Part of him may have wanted to open up, but the other half remained closed. Margie's heart broke. She could only hope he'd let out his feelings instead of keeping them locked up inside. His physical body was healing; it was the mental and emotional side of him that needed an intervention.

Margie glanced at Pastor Benson whose closed eyes told her he was praying. She joined him in lending a short silent prayer asking God for discernment. The words, *she didn't deserve it...I had to do it*, hung in the air. *What did he have to do?*

Everyone knew for a while of Jason's addiction. Margie understood from the experience of others she'd counseled in the past that there was a deep emotional attachment to whatever caused substance abuse. Also, she knew Jason had a stubborn spot for sharing his true feelings. How many young twenty-somethings displayed the same tough-guy persona when inside they were gentle as lambs? They needed only prodding in the right direction to rid themselves of the emotional baggage that weighed them down. Sometimes, it could take forever. Sometimes not. She believed Jason had a sensitive heart. She saw the way he used to help the elderly at church and the compassion he'd shown toward children during the summertime Bible Fun Day when he helped out with leading some of the games. That was all before he started to do drugs. Could things have changed that much? She held out hope that nothing had altered too drastically that God couldn't repair.

"Jason?" Pastor Benson began. "Talk to me, son. About your mother. You said you had to *do it*?"

Margie mentally questioned the association with his mother and wondered why the boy had brought her up. She knew Pastor had spoken with Becca before about Jason, but who could believe the boy could be capable of burning his parents' house down? Even on his worst day, the young man didn't have that kind of mean streak. There was something else bothering him, something deeper than just twenty-something angst.

Jason pulled his face from the pillow. He wiped his reddened eyes with the back of his hand and shifted under the bedsheet. He drew in a breath. "I...I never...."

Margie wanted to speak up. She understood the difficulty in sharing the pain of a long-buried hurt to someone, whether a shrink, a counselor, or even a Sunday School teacher. Even more so, she believed there could be only one person to bear this kind of burden to at time. Opening up to more than one set of ears would be too much like an interrogation.

"Pastor, I'm going to wait out in the hall." She pointed to the doorway and then turned to Jason. "I'm going to leave you here alone with Pastor, Jason. I just want you to know how much we care about you—everyone does." She patted his arm reassuringly and left the room.

Margie paced the long hallway. Just beyond the last room, she paused to look out the window at the end of the corridor. The image of the little infant she'd found in the woods hovered in her mind. Distant trees stood protectively around the park where the baby had been heartlessly discarded. She ached at the thought of someone abandoning the precious life. Hopefully, the baby was doing well.

On her way back down the hall, she paused as two orderlies maneuvered a patient's bed out of one of the rooms. She stepped aside to let them pass. Near the threshold to Jason's room, she stopped.

The late afternoon sunlight poured brightly into the room. Margie caught a glimpse of Pastor Benson holding his Bible and letting the soft, onion-skin-paper ripple as he fanned the pages with his fingers. Then Jason spoke.

"I've never told anyone, not a soul—ever."

His words piqued her curiosity, and she turned an ear into the room.

"I understand," the pastor assured.

Moments later, Margie thought she heard the words, *I killed my father.*

Chapter Twenty-Five

The words landed no less devastatingly than a bomb. Margie's insides quaked at the shocking revelation. Did she hear correctly? She inched closer to the door and peeked her head around. The pastor still stood at the side of the bed. At this angle, she could see part of pastor's back and most of Jason's face.

"Go on," Pastor said with a nod. "I'm listening."

"My *real* father," he said, his voice low. "It was an accident, though. I never intended any harm—I swear." Jason's guileless expression said it all. The pain in his eyes was evident. *This boy was no killer.* Pastor appeared unfazed. Yet, she couldn't tell for sure with his back to her. He either believed Jason's testimony or he didn't. She braced herself for the rest of what Jason would say.

"How did this happen, son?"

The room grew quiet. Margie strained to hear. A minute went by and she wondered why Jason suddenly went mum. She waited in the momentary, subdued hush of the hallway, and then he began speaking.

"It was the summer I turned eighteen." He paused. "Up in the mountains. It was my mom's idea after some counselor suggested to send me away for a while...to get my head straight or something."

"How did you take it? Resentful, glad?"

Jason shrugged. "Can't remember, really."

"Tell me more about the stay up in...where was this again?"

"Up in the mountains in Kempton...stayed with old family friends—Joe and Lois Ferrier. She was my mom's best friend forever, and they needed a helping hand around the campground and all."

"Where does your father fit into this?"

"One day, I was doing some yard work, and I heard someone call my name. I turned around and there he was—my father. Thought I was seeing a ghost or something. Like he'd just been beamed in—from hell."

"Were you frightened—or?"

"Well, I guess, shocked. I mean, I hadn't seen him in years. We all thought he'd died. Drank himself to death, maybe." He shook his head. "That was what they told me—Aunt Marie and everyone."

"So, what happened next?"

"At first, I did a double take and all. He looked different than how I remembered him, but it was obviously him. He put his arm around me like we were best buds."

"So, all was good then, I assume?"

Jason cast his gaze down and answered, "For a while, yeah, but..." He paused. "Then we went for a walk."

Pastor Benson leaned forward as though on the verge of a breakthrough.

"We walked up to the top of Hawk Mountain. That's where everyone goes to watch birds and all."

Pastor nodded. "Yes, I'm familiar with it. Beautiful place."

"At some time when we were walking, he started talking about my mom. Later on, he said something mean about her. Called her a bitch or something like that." He clenched his fist and rubbed it absently against his bandaged right-hand wrist. "I suddenly saw red. I couldn't believe I was hearing those words from him about my mother. I knew he was lying through his teeth."

Jason's face drew taut. He looked away from Pastor Benson and stared somewhere out the window. Outside the doorway, Margie prayed the confession would lend a cathartic effect. Like opening up a festering wound, once the poison is out, the body can begin to heal.

Pastor Benson stood patiently and said, "Did you say anything to him? Challenge him?"

Jason cast his gaze back to pastor. "He was going on about something she did...we were on a steep path by then—almost to the top of the mountain. But I got sore at him, real sore." He paused and ran his good hand down the back of his head. "I wanted so much to punch him really hard just to get him to stop. I was angry and sweltering in the heat by then. Not in the mood for his crap. I mean it was pissing me off big-time." He flung his hand to his face. "Oh, God, why am I telling you all this?" He slapped his good arm down on the bed and then grabbed himself by the neck and smirked. "They must have me really doped up for sure."

"It's okay, son. Please continue."

After a long pause, he said, "Well, you know the rest."

"I can only imagine," Pastor said, softly.

"I just—just got so freakin' angry. He wouldn't shut up after I defended her, he just poo-pooed it like I didn't know what I was talking about..." His words trailed. His mouth drew into a straight line. "I punched him. So hard that he lost his balance and fell backwards. He rolled and rolled. The incline was steep and—" His features crumpled.

Jason covered his face with his good hand. Pastor stood stoically while allowing the information to settle and then walked around to the other side of Jason's bed nearer the window.

"He fell so far down. It was a sheer drop, at least two hundred feet, probably more. I didn't know what to do. I couldn't reach him. I knew he didn't survive." His words came out fast, laced with emotion. "He had to have hit his head on any one of a hundred rocks or boulders along the way." Jason raised his good hand in frustration and helplessly let it drop back onto the sheet. "I didn't even hit him that hard...just slugged him." He rocked his head in his hand. "I didn't mean to kill him!" Jason wailed. "I panicked. So, I just ran—ran back to the campground, grabbed my stuff, and bolted away as fast as I could."

And you've never stopped running, Margie thought. *Running away from the memories...never getting far. Filling up on drugs to dim the remembrance, ease the pain.*

When Jason stopped rocking, he confessed, "Pastor, I've never told anyone about any of this before." He wiped his eyes with his good arm. "You're the only person."

Pastor gave him an efficient smile. "I'm honored, Jason. Truly I am. That you would confide in me these devastating and hurtful memories you've been holding inside." He pursed his lips together and then nodded. "It took a lot of guts, young man. And please remember"—he palmed his chest over his heart — "what you shared will remain with me and only me. Not to worry." He moved closer to the bed. Taking Jason's hand, he asked, "May I pray with you, son?"

Pastor Benson said a prayer and then picked up his suit jacket from the back of the chair. "You've made great progress here today. Soon as you get out of the hospital and rehab, I'm sure your life will take a new path if you put the Lord first. Be sure, we'll be praying for you and Lark."

The pastor raised the palm of his hand and stepped away from the bed. He picked up his Bible and turned to leave.

Chapter Twenty-Six

Becca's breath caught in an untethered fear that something was wrong. Her thoughts darted like fireflies. As far as she knew, Miss Bea had never left the apartment before when babysitting Tally. This was the first time. Why would she have had to leave?

Every news outlet on the internet relayed story after story lately of people going missing from even the most innocuous places. Unlike the time of her youth, the blissful days of being naïve to terror were over. After reading about the girl who'd been taken from her bedroom—the famous story about Elizabeth Smart years ago—it seemed to Becca that evil in the world crept closer to the forefront. The headlines blazed of local incidents right in the Philadelphia area with everyday people having ill will thrust upon their lives. The Joan Bledsoe case...Amy Goodman... the mother-daughter incident in a parking garage over a Louis Vuitton handbag. A sinking feeling hit the pit of her stomach.

Becca scanned the complex again. Commuters along the road adjacent to the property passed by as though everything were normal. Right now, she'd trade places with any one of them. Mrs. Holder stood behind an oversized blue stroller and wheeled it down the walkway by the *D* section of apartments. Across the courtyard, Gus, the handyman, carried a bucket and mop into the maintenance shed.

Where were Miss Bea and Tally? Then it hit. In her haste, Becca hadn't even thought of going to Miss Bea's apartment down the hall. Of course, that's where they were! Becca raced back down the walkway to *Building A* and ran into the mailman along the way.

"Hi, Ms. Wallace, got some mail for you." He reached into her mailbox and pulled out a white envelope.

"Oh, hi, Dave." She rushed by, never understanding why mailmen couldn't just leave her mail inside the box. They always wanted to hand it over if she were around while they were sorting and distributing. It was a nice gesture, but it wasn't like she'd won the sweepstakes or anything. Odds are, it was just a bill. It could wait. "Thanks." She waved the air between them. "I'll get it later."

He raised an inquisitive eyebrow.

"Well, on second thought." She grabbed the envelope from his outstretched hand and double-timed it back down the hallway.

As she approached Miss Bea's apartment, the door swiftly swung open, and the elderly lady rushed out, running into Becca. Her doe-like eyes were soaked with tears and punctuated with fear.

"Miss Becca," the woman sobbed.

Becca's stomach lurched in anticipation of what she was about to say.

"Oh, Miss Becca, they took her!"

"Took her? Took Tally?" Her bowels dropped.

"Tally, they took her!" she repeated.

"Miss Bea, who's *they*?"

The woman's stunned expression bore the likes of a frightened animal. Her hands shook as she explained what had happened while babysitting Tally.

"They-they come to door," she said. "Lady and tall man. And just walk inside. I turn around and she have Tally. She take her out—with dolly and bag. That's it. Gone." Her palms flew to her face. She cupped her cheeks and shook her head regretfully.

Becca reached to console the woman and took her hands and held them. "Miss Bea, tell me, what did they look like? The people who took Tally."

Miss Bea hesitated and then described the woman who'd come for Tally. "Tall." She raised her hand in the air. "Dark hair." She pulled a strand of her own that fell across her face.

"That's all you remember?" Becca's hands trembled. "A woman and a man?"

She nodded. "I try to call you—no answer, Miss Becca. I'm so sorry," she said as her face folded.

Becca's stomach twisted as she observed the scene unfold in her head. *Was Children and Youth Services responsible for this? Did they send someone out to take Tally away?* She flinched inwardly as an icy fear struck. *Or Athena? Or worse, were they kidnappers?*

"Please don't cry, Miss Bea. It's not your fault." Becca consoled the woman and put on a brave front. Having to comfort Miss Bea all while her precious granddaughter was missing—or kidnapped—brought her to the brink. Right then, she needed support more than anyone.

While consoling Miss Bea, Becca's words sounded hollow in her ears as though someone else said them through a long funnel. She comforted her the best she could, but the woman was inconsolable. It took a while for Miss Bea to comprehend the situation and that it did not reflect on her protective skills or any negligence on her part. As Becca ministered to Miss Bea, her own heart strained within. *Who could have done this? Who would want to take Tally?*

Becca summoned an inner confidence and all the while hoped Paul would be home soon. Paul, her anchor. He'd be able to sort things out and would know what to do. Right now, she needed him more than ever. She was fast approaching the precipice of her sanity.

Chapter Twenty-Seven

"We've lost custody," Becca announced the minute Paul came through the door. She hated bombing him with bad news before he'd even had a chance to take his shoes off and relax a bit. She waved the letter from Children and Youth Services. "It says 'we regret to inform you that your Foster Kinship term has ended.'"

"What?" Paul shot back.

"That's what it says." She poked the paper with her index finger.

"Let me see it." He motioned with his hand and took a seat at the table.

"Right here." She pointed to the sentence.

"What are they talking about?" He pored over the page.

Becca peered over his shoulder. "I can't believe this. Are they insane?"

"Shhh, let me read, Bec." He waved his hand irritably. "Hold on."

We regret to inform you that your Foster Kinship Program term has ended...the court under the jurisdiction of Judge John Lazinsky has ruled...care will be handled by a foster parent yet to be decided, and when forthcoming, you will be notified. For now, please be advised that all care of Tally Ann Wallace is under the guidance and supervision of CYS... all responsibilities, personal or otherwise, are no longer contingent or dependent upon you, and you are now officially released from all further parental law pursuant to this...

"What the—!" Paul yelled.

"I know. What the heck are they talking about? First of all, don't they need a warrant to take a child out of her home? Oh, for Pete's sake, this is total insanity."

"That explains her whereabouts," Paul said. "At least, we know—"

"Her whereabouts?" she cried. "We don't know where she is, Paul, or who she's with."

"But she's *safe* Bec, she's with the County. I'm sure they'll be able to place her somewhere. They're not going to leave her out in the street." His measured tone took some of the sting out, but her anger remained intact.

"But where? Why'd they have to take her?" Becca silently sobbed into her hands. Taking in the harsh words was like swallowing nails. They'd popped on the page like daggers. *How dare they. After three years of faithfully tending to the child, this is the thanks we get?* She wanted to rip the letter into shreds and burn it. "We never did anything but the right thing by her—ever. Always on time to pick her up at Athena's. Always dressed her beautifully. Gave her the world. I mean, look around. We bought half the stuff in the apartment for *her*."

Becca cast her gaze around and took in the toys, games, and dollhouse in the corner of the living room because Tally's bedroom was too small to house all of her things. She mused on all of the extra-curricular activities where she was enrolled—T-ball, ballet, swim lessons...everything she and Paul provided. Their undying love was the bow on top of the package. "I mean, she was happy here, right?" Becca wiped her eyes.

"Of course, she was," he answered. "No doubt about it."

In a huff, she jerked away from the table and marched out of the room.

"Where are you going?"

"I'm getting to the bottom of this."

"How?"

"I don't know," she yelled from the hall as she headed for the bedroom. "But I will. You'll see. They can't treat us like this. We've done nothing wrong. What infringement or negligence or whatever the Sam Hill they're ticked off about is baloney."

"Want me to make my own dinner?" he called down the hall.

Becca couldn't believe he was concerned with food at a time like this. With a sigh, she said, "Go ahead. I'm not hungry." She restrained herself from saying any more, lest she lash out at him.

"Hon, it's not forever," Paul said, now at the threshold to their room. "Maybe there was a glitch in the system. This could be just a mistake. You know how bureaucracies are. So big and so many times inefficient."

Becca could see he was trying his hardest to soothe her hurt. She loved him for it. But right now, there was no panacea for her wounded pride. "I don't know, but I think I know what *may* have happened," she said.

Paul's eyes crinkled with curiosity. "How's that?"

"Tuesday, the day of the hearing...a couple of weeks ago." She sat down on the bed and stroked the soft nap of the comforter up and down with her palm.

"Yeah."

"There's something that happened when I was there."

"What happened?"

"I had words with the judge."

"Huh?" He gave her a quizzical look. "What kind of words?"

"I needed to get it off my chest, there was no holding it in... like a volcano about to explode, so—"

"So, did you..." Paul said, filling in her sentence, "...explode?"

Chagrined, Becca nodded. "Yep."

He scrunched up his face. "What happened? I thought you said the hearing was closed."

"It was." She twisted a stray wisp of hair. "But I kind of snuck into the back of the courtroom while the hearing was going on and hung out."

"Kind of? So, where or when did you have words?"

She folded her knees up to her chest. "In the courtroom."

"The courtroom?"

"I had an outburst." She lowered her head. "I regret it now, but it's been welling up in me ever since Margie told me about a picture Athena showed her. A picture of Lark and a man. She said it looked, I don't know, kind of incriminating."

"Like...?" He raised an eyebrow.

"Exactly," she quipped, reading his thoughts. His daughter-in-law had been cheating.

"So, what did you say?"

"I just called her out."

"Who?"

"Lark, who else?"

"In front of everyone or privately?"

"Right out loud."

"Without the attorney?"

"No, he was there."

"What did he say?"

"What could he say? Oh, you mean afterward?"

"Yes, afterward."

"He was kind of upset with me."

Paul threw his hands up. "I'm sure he was. What would prompt you to do that, Becca?"

Becca chafed at the sharpness in his voice. "Don't get mad at me, too, Paul."

"I don't know what to tell you, Becca."

"Why are you mad at me? I mean, I'm fighting for us to get custody, and all the while I have to fight City Hall and Lark and now you?" Her voice pitched.

"I'm not mad at you, I'm mad at the situation," he argued. He paced across the room.

"Well, I'm not so sure," she muttered under her breath.

"What?"

"Nothing," she snapped. She didn't want to exacerbate the situation, though her emotions screamed to get out. "I just thought for sure that she was two-timing my son by having an affair, so I had to say something. And I did."

Paul silently brooded. The tension in the room thickened with both of them on either side of a great divide. She hated when they fought like this. He may not have been mad at her, but the darts of his anger pelted her nonetheless. It would be better to get their feelings out and clear the air, like a bandage ripped off quickly instead of excruciatingly slow, than to conduct this cat-and-mouse game where the argument dragged on for hours. Their fighting was a rare occurrence, but right now she didn't need the added aggravation of wondering whether or not he was on her side. If she'd made a mistake in erupting at the hearing, there was nothing she could do about it now.

An unbearable weight of fatigue filled her limbs. She undressed and put on her nightshirt.

"I'm going to bed," she said. She pulled back the bedsheets. "I can't deal with any more today." Drained, she climbed into bed and barely noticed the cool softness of the new, smooth cotton sheets for all of the mixed thoughts and emotions coursing through her.

Her body needed rest, but her mind remained wired. She prepared a game plan and played out the scenes in her mind of what she'd like to do. The County overstepped its bounds as far as she was concerned. This would not be the way things would be, and she would not take the letter sitting down or let them trounce over her and Paul. The plan she devised ran like a film reel on replay, a continuous loop in her head.

"Bec?" Paul softly tapped his finger on her exposed shoulder.

She feigned sleep.

"Bec?"

"What?" she said into the pillow, her curiosity getting the better of her.

"I don't think we should go to bed mad at each other. I'm just as miserable about this as you are." He paused. "I'm sorry."

She opened one eye and saw his face etched in little-boy guilt and was grateful that he hadn't emotionally abandoned her.

"Let's pray." Paul sat down on the bed as she rolled over. He reached for her hand.

As Paul prayed, her thoughts drifted to the situation with the authorities, and her fears about Tally escalated again. *Did she have her pajamas? Her toothbrush? Did they know she was gluten-sensitive? Safety aside, who was she staying with?* She silently poured her heart out to God once more that he'd watch over their granddaughter and give them wisdom on how to handle the circumstances that right now were out of control.

Chapter Twenty-Eight

In the middle of the night, Becca tossed in a fitful sleep. When she awoke, she clung to the hope her beloved grandaughter was safe in her new surroundings. She got up and padded down to Tally's room and laid herself down on the bed where she cried herself back to sleep. When she awoke, fear took over again. She worried that she'd never find out where they took Tally. The absence of the little girl left a vacuum in her wake.

The sun crept up and the room flooded with light. She desperately needed to call the County. On the verge of placing the call, she hesitated, fearful of how she'd approach them. If she'd lost custody because of her sudden outburst in the courtroom, it wouldn't surprise her that they might very well put a temporary restraining order on her, or worse, a permanent one. Instead, she called Athena to share what had happened.

****

"Say, what?" the woman exclaimed. "Those bastards."

Athena sounded shocked at hearing about Tally's disappearance and claimed she had no idea of the child's whereabouts. Though, during the call, Becca's high-alert radar kicked in. Was this just a ploy? She tried to find a loophole in the woman's ardent defense that she didn't know where Tally was. She could have taken Tally, Becca thought. It was a distinct possibly that Athena had taken her or had someone else do it, but she wasn't sure. On one hand, the idea was ludicrous. On the other, anything was possible.

Becca's past instincts weren't as finely tuned as they were now, and for the longest time she had completely trusted people.

Never wanting to rock the boat too much, she'd silently amended others' bad behavior and willingly accepted it as her lot. One day, she could no longer accept the paint-by-numbers picture she'd created for her life with her first husband. It left her in pieces when she finally understood how far he fell short of a good husband—or a husband at all. How naïve she had been. The hours crawled by as though weighted by stone. Praying helped dilute the grief, but nothing could distract her from the image of Tally's face.

The following morning, Becca awoke, her head thick in a cerebral fog. At first, she couldn't think straight and panicked when Paul wasn't anywhere in the apartment. Then she realized he had gone to work. She got up and put on the same jeans from the previous day and wondered how long she could keep up with the nightmare that was now her life.

Every day, Becca anxiously waited for the mailman to arrive, desperate for news—any news—about Tally. The living room of the apartment was adjacent to the hallway, where if any movement came, she could hear it through the thin wall. She grew keen with anticipation of his arrival, eager for the sound of his jingling key that opened up the row of mailboxes. Like a child waiting for Santa Claus, she listened while he stuffed envelopes and packages into the compartments. The moment he left, she raced out the door, key in hand, to open the skinny gray box.

Today, she found three pieces of mail: a supermarket flyer, a utility bill from the electric company, and a white envelope with the return address of Children and Youth Services. Her heart kicked into overdrive. She tore open the letter and skimmed each line quickly. Her heart skipped when toward the bottom it mentioned the foster family's address: *667 Briarthorn Drive, Mount St. Clair, PA*. She searched for the name of the foster parents, but the letter didn't reveal it. Nothing lent a clue as to who they were, only that they lived on the far side of the county.

She darted back inside and turned on the computer. Normally, she'd check her email first thing, but something else was on her mind this morning. With the computer up and running, she clicked on Google Earth and plugged in the address: *667 Briarthorn Drive* and waited for the computer to process the information. She'd done searches before—places like Niagara Falls and the Great Pyramids. As breathtaking as the sites were, seeing where her granddaughter now lived dwarfed even the Grand Canyon. The virtual camera moved at her command, allowing her to hone in like a laser onto the street. Single-family homes—colonials and ranch-styled houses comprised most of the neighborhood, along with a few saltboxes on what appeared to be quarter-acre lots. A large open field, possibly farmland, took up the area across the street from 667. Her pulse ticked faster as she panned the camera across the street and up to the house. She bubbled with excitement at the thought of seeing Tally somewhere on the property.

The modest white house had black shutters. Landscape plantings were minimal. A large tree stood in the front yard by a wooden split-rail fence. She studied the scene until it seared her brain. *Lord, please keep her safe.*

****

"Hey, Jane, it's me."

"Hey, there. You sound like you're in a good mood. Any word yet?"

"Sort of. The letter from the County came."

"Oh, that's great...finally. What'd they say?"

"I found the address. It's in Mount St. Clair."

"Really? That's not too far away," Jane said. "Feeling better now?"

"I guess. A little, I suppose. But I have some thoughts about it. Actually, I've got a plan."

"Sounds serious. What is it?"

"Can you do lunch...say, today?"

"Absolutely. Nothing on the docket today except a hair appointment at four."

"Okay, good. Let's meet at the pizza place at the mall. Is that good for you?"

"Sure thing. What time is good, noonish?"

"Perfect. See you then."

Chapter Twenty-Nine

The church's long-term renovation project was finally completed. The adjacent parking lot, coated in newly poured black asphalt, lent a freshness to the property. Long gone was the clutter of the backhoe and all of the other construction trappings—work benches, tools, and equipment that occupied the area outside the church for weeks on end.

Pastor Benson pulled up to the church just before nine o'clock. Margie hadn't arrived yet; her bright orange Volkswagen was usually the first car in the lot in the morning. Everyone teased her that she drove a tangerine.

Inside, the hallway leading to his office gleamed in freshly painted eggshell-colored walls and complementary beige-brown carpeting. Margie had done a good job coordinating all of the contractors, and the fruits of their labor would be evident to everyone come this Sunday. The pastor made sure she put an announcement in the bulletin to thank everyone for their generous financial support of the renovation project.

Pastor Benson pulled out a key and opened his office door. He placed his bagged lunch inside the mini fridge and hung his suit jacket on the back of his door. A piece of paper lay on his chair, a note from Margie: *Just a reminder that I won't be in today. I'm working from home to get the Welcome Wagon baskets together. See you bright and early Tuesday. Blessings, Margie.*

****

Becca pulled open the door to the restaurant. The sweet aroma of simmering herb-infused tomato sauce permeated the air.

"Table for one?" the young woman behind the counter asked.

"Not yet, I'm waiting for someone, thanks," Becca replied. She picked up one of the menus from the stack by the cash register and took a step to the side. She hadn't eaten so well in the past few days, but today everything on the menu looked good. She perused the selections and settled on a personal-size plain pizza and salad. She put the menu back and continued to wait. One by one, the lunch crowd filtered in; first, a couple of guys in business suits and then two ladies followed. Right behind them came Jane.

****

At the table, Jane looked searchingly at her friend. "Okay, so what's this about..."—Jane made air quotes— "a *plan*?"

Becca put down her glass and folded her arms on the edge of the table. "Okay, but this is just between you and me."

"Absolutely."

"No husbands, no anybody."

"Got it. No problem."

"So, I've been thinking and praying, and—"

"Here you go," the server said as she arrived with their food and set them on the table, beginning with Jane's margherita pizza and French onion soup, followed by Becca's plain pizza and garden salad with French dressing on the side.

"Anything else I can get you ladies?" The perky waitress folded the serving tray under her arm.

Jane busily shook hot pepper flakes onto her pizza, and Becca replied, "I think we're okay, thanks." Then to Jane, she said, "And like I was saying, I'm still not one hundred percent it's a good idea. I'm on the fence."

"I'm listening," Jane said, picking up a slice.

During the meal, Becca spelled out the details of what she had in mind.

"You really want to do this?" Jane spoke in between bites. "Sounds daring."

"Sure," Becca said. "What's the harm?" She picked up the last slice of pizza and took a bite.

"It's just... I mean, how do you figure it'll work out?"

Becca swallowed and wordlessly responded with a shrug and took another bite.

"Look, I'm with you, Bec. I am. It just feels like—oh, I don't know—"

"Voyeurism?" Becca said through a mouthful.

"Yeah, I guess."

The idea of driving to Mount St. Clair and spying on the home where her granddaughter was staying sounded ridiculous at first. Though the more she dwelled on it, the more the idea appealed to her.

"It sounds like an *I Love Lucy* episode." Jane grinned.

"If my life were a comedy, I could see your point," Becca replied, flatly.

Jane's mouth arched downward. "Oh, Bec, I didn't mean to make light of the situation."

"No, no. I'm fine."

"I'm still sorry...sorry that you're going through this."

"It's okay."

"So, when do you plan on doing it?"

Becca's stomach danced at the thought of actually going through with the plan. She hadn't figured on a time or a date. It was just an idea, and just talking out loud about it was enough for now. Even though she'd go to the moon and back to see Tally, it would take some extraordinary courage to follow through with what she had in mind. The full truth of her plan she hadn't shared with anyone yet. Not even Jane. For now, it would be one step at a time.

Chapter Thirty

The image of a tiny child floated in the air and peeked out from the clouds. The child seemed to be calling Becca, first from above and then below. A ball of silver yarn attached itself to Becca's ankle as she dangled over a precipitous mountain gorge. Below, a raging river flowed downstream where an empty raft floated. The unraveling thread took her lower and lower into a dark abyss. Tally was there, too, along with another child, and they called for her to join them. The startling images threatened her in one form or another, and she yearned to reach Tally but was always an arm's length away.

Becca awakened with a jolt. She turned over and laid her hand on Paul's side of the bed. The coolness of his pillow indicated he'd gotten up a while ago. She vaguely recalled him talking to her earlier and then felt his lips or something wet on her cheek. He must have gone to work. She hadn't told him anything about her plans about canvassing the neighborhood where Tally was supposedly staying. If she had, he might have deterred her from doing it. *Where would it lead?* he'd say to her. *Better stay away, it could be illegal.*

Always keeping vigilant and bound by the straight and narrow, Paul, fifteen years her senior, represented a godly example of a man, who didn't straddle the fence for anything. She was reticent, at first, to marry him, but soon he swept her up and, in time, love blossomed. She learned to trust again. Having Tally in their lives had been another bloom added to her bouquet. But now, the flowers were fading fast, and their absence left the vase of her heart empty.

****

Becca drove down the side streets through her former neighborhood and turned onto Scarlet Oak Lane. Tears welled in her eyes. Their old house, still holding its own amid the rubble and boarded up windows, stood as a reminder of that fateful day when the fire destroyed it. The charred shutters and burnt clapboard broke her spirit. When she and Paul had joined with other churches back in 2006 and traveled to Louisiana to help the Hurricane Katrina victims, the devastation she saw back then wrenched her heart. Now, she bore the same feeling as she drove down Scarlet Oak Lane. Only this time, she suffered double the heartache because the damaged structure was her own home.

Jane stood outside by the curb and waved as Becca pulled up.

Becca hit the button to roll down the window. "Morning," she called out.

"Morning," Jane replied. An intoxicating blend of jasmine and gardenia floated with her as she hopped onto the front seat. She placed her handbag on the floor, kept the water bottle on her lap, and buckled herself in.

"Ready for the adventure?" Becca released the brake and took one last glance at her old house as she pulled away.

Jane grinned. "Feels like Cagney and Lacy." She adjusted the brim of her baseball cap.

Becca smiled inwardly. She had never staked out anyone's house before, and, yes, it did feel like a TV drama. "I've never seen you wear a hat before," Becca said.

"I'm trying to disguise myself."

"We're only driving by the house."

"No, my roots." She pointed to her head. "They need touching up."

"Oh, never mind." Becca chuckled.

****

The home sat in a small enclave in Mount St. Clair, a blend of modest and established old-money homes on the other side of the county. As they made their way along the leafy, tree-lined streets, misty fog blanketed the air. It lent a moodiness to the otherwise upscale community and, to Becca, bore all the makings of a B-movie right before the boogeyman popped out from behind the bushes.

Jane reached inside her purse and pulled out her glasses. "What's the address we're looking for?"

"Briarthorn, 667 Briarthorn Drive."

"What street are we on now?"

"Still on Hickory Lane, I think. No, wait." Becca craned her neck to read the street sign. "Okay, this is Summer Hill. It should turn into Heritage in another block or two."

"So, where's Briarthorn?"

"If I have my bearings, it shouldn't be too much farther...right off of Heritage."

"Did you do a Mapquest search?"

"Sure did, but I forgot to bring the directions." She flicked her finger against her head. "So dumb. Doesn't matter, though. I studied the map for so long, it's ingrained." She glanced at Jane. "It's my obsession."

"Why wouldn't it be? You love your granddaughter."

When Becca first inspected the foster home online via the Mapquest feature, she wondered what kind of people were now taking care of Tally. As she zoomed in on the property and the surrounding homes in the neighborhood, she anticipated seeing a glimpse of Tally. Although, in her heart, she knew it to be only a pipe dream; for all anyone knew, the online satellite images could have been captured months or even years before. Despite the urgency to see her granddaughter, seeing the house did not comfort her as much as she had hoped. It wasn't enough. The vicarious trip only reinforced her desire to go there in person. The sooner the better.

Becca's anxiety rose with each passing street. "I'm getting nervous." She flipped the AC vent directly onto her face.

"You'll be okay," Jane said. "Is it coming up soon?"

"Any minute now. Just beyond Larkspur Lane should be Briarthorn. Yep, here it is."

She tapped the brakes and slowly made the turn onto Briarthorn Drive. The beauty of the two-story stone facades of the homes along the first block resembled a real estate brochure.

"People actually live here?" Jane stared in disbelief as they cruised down the street. "How can anyone afford these McMansions? The electricity bills must be sky high."

"I don't know," Becca replied. "Maybe they're Ponzi schemers or trust fund babies."

"Must be nice."

"It's coming up," Becca announced as she crept up the street. Her heart thumped.

"Where?" Jane questioned. "That one?" She pointed to a two-story colonial with cornflower-blue shutters.

"No, next door. The white one."

Becca pulled to the curb and idled the engine while her gaze fixed on the property. The white clapboard cottage with black shutters appeared modest compared to the other homes in the neighborhood. A rutted asphalt driveway led the way up a slight incline to the home, and behind it sat a two-car garage. A large shade tree stood off to the side. The front had a couple of anemic looking bushes under the first-floor windows. A weathered split-rail fence surrounded the front yard, and the backyard fencing consisted of the standard gray chain-link.

"Nice neighborhood," Jane said. She panned her gaze in a 180-degree turn. "So quiet."

Becca agreed and nodded absently, thinking that if there were children in the neighborhood, they'd probably be in school right now, and Tally would still be enrolled at the Chester Springs Day

& KinderKare if she hadn't been taken away. A stab of grief cut into her. *Why, Lord? What's the purpose in all of this?*

She sat transfixed and stared out the window. While the house was an innocent bystander in the war going on inside her, she loathed it and wanted to erase its image from the neighborhood… the crumbling driveway, the leggy bushes. The clapboard house was ridiculously small compared to the adjacent tree that was oversized for the yard. The structure didn't fit into the neighborhood any more than Tally did.

One by one, Becca ticked off the annoyances as she saw them. All the while, she held on fast that at any moment, Tally could come running out of the house just as she'd done numerous times after staying at Athena's. She'd hurry down the steps and rush right into Becca's arms. Becca ached inside. It wouldn't happen today—or probably ever again.

Tally, are you inside?

Becca checked every window for a glimpse of her granddaughter. Could she be playing dolls in her room? Or hanging out back in the yard? From this angle, she couldn't tell whether there was a swing set or anything of interest to a five-year-old going on six at the foster house. Were there other children inside? Did the foster parents take in others that Tally could play with? Was she being homeschooled? The questions circled in Becca's head.

"Looks like you're a mile away."

"Sorry, just thinking is all."

"I'm sure. Hey, what do you think of that car? Could it be any more orange?" Jane snorted a laugh as she pointed out the window.

Becca eyed the car parked at the bottom of the driveway. "Whoa, that looks like *Margie's* car."

"The lady I met at the courthouse…dark hair?"

"Yeah, what's she doing here?" Becca stretched her neck to get a better look through the smudged windshield. "I'd know her car anywhere. That's gotta be hers. Who else would drive a car the color of a tangerine?"

Becca recalled the time when Margie needed a car and put an announcement in the church bulletin. Her preference was a pre-owned or inexpensive one. At some point later, she began driving a late model Volkswagen. She nicknamed it Miss Tang.

"This is so weird. I wonder what's going on?" Becca said, eyeing the car, still hoping it was just another orange VW.

"Unless it's someone else's car."

"That color? I don't think so."

They sat in silence. Becca was glad the neighborhood was more upscale than Athena's and didn't appear as though drug dealers would be drawn to linger on the corners any time soon. Although, one could never be too sure. She recalled the surprising and quite unbelievable news in high school when someone told her that Darren Pronchuck, the tenth grade class president and Miss Adams' teacher's pet, had sold marijuana from his bedroom window.

Now that she saw the house, it didn't lessen her grief. She wouldn't rest until she knew the child was okay—both physically and emotionally. She ached to tell her that she and her grandfather hadn't abandoned her. She longed to see Tally more than ever.

What in the world would Margie be doing at the new foster family's home?

Something wasn't right. Seeing Margie's car parked there now gave Becca something else to worry about.

The moments ticked by, and both her palms as well as her underarms had grown moist. She knew Margie wanted a child of her own; it was no secret to her or anyone in the church. When Margie had lost her first child in miscarriage and then had to deal with her husband's death while he'd served in the military, she received a double shot of heartbreak. It was hard to witness the woman's emotional pain. Margie's wounds had taken a while to heal and kept her in a depressed mood for a long time.

Becca's thoughts raced. *Could Margie have taken Tally?* In her desperation, did Margie want a child so badly that she'd become a foster parent? Becca couldn't fathom it.

Jane poked around the bottom of her purse, and the sound of crackling paper filled the quiet car. "Want a peanut butter cracker?" she asked.

Becca's gaze remained fixed as she studied the house. The words Jane had spoken didn't register.

"Bec?" Jane held up the crackers.

"Oh, no, I'm good but thanks." Becca waved the offer away. Food was the furthest thing from her mind. All she could consume right now were her exaggerated thoughts about why Margie of all people would be here. And where was Tally?

Out of the corner of her eye, movement came from around the side of the house. Becca strained for a better look, but the vehicle at the top of the driveway partially obscured the view.

"I think there's something..."

"What is it?"

"Not sure...thought I saw someone." Becca craned her neck over the console. A moment later, she cringed. The shock stabbed her gut. *I can't believe this!*

"Hold on, isn't that your friend Margie?"

"Looks like it," Becca said.

"She's talking to a guy. I guess that's the foster father? Wait, what? Looks like he's carrying her over the threshold like they just got married. What's that about?"

Becca squinted. She needed new glasses, but for now, the picture was crystal clear. The man held Margie in his arms. One arm circled around her waist, and the other he cradled underneath her legs. She wore casual clothes—black slacks and a red, short-sleeved blouse. Blood rushed to Becca's face. Through the overgrown bushes by the neighbor's driveway, she watched him carry Margie down the driveway.

"What in the world...?"

As the couple neared the street and got closer to Margie's car, Becca quickly turned her head away, not wanting to be recognized. "What are they doing now?" she asked Jane in a forced whisper.

"They're just talking." Jane lowered the visor and peeked out from behind it. "She's in the car, and he's just standing there. He just closed her door. Hey, I've seen that guy before."

"You have?"

"Yes."

"Where?"

"I'm pretty sure I saw him at your house."

"*My* house? Really, when? Are you sure?" Becca's curiosity took over and she turned back in time to see a glimpse of the man from the back as he hustled up the driveway. "Dang, I couldn't get a good look at him." She banged her hand on the wheel. "So, when was this?"

"Was it this summer?" Jane mused out loud. "No, no. Not this summer—it must have been last summer. I remember seeing him talking with Lark one day out back by the fence."

"Did you hear anything? Do you know what they were talking about?"

"Not really. I was busy getting ready to do some gardening. I wasn't paying much attention, really."

"So, you say he was at my house?" Becca scoured her memory of who it possibly could have been.

Jane shrugged. "I guess it was one of your daughter-in-law's friends. He looked pretty dejected when he left."

"Hmmm," Becca said.

Just then, Margie pulled out and drove away.

"What do you make of it? I can see your mind processing something, Bec. By the way you don't look so hot. You okay? You look pale."

Becca glanced in the rearview mirror. "I've felt better, but I'll be all right," she said, trying to convince herself as a feeling of faintness came over her.

"You better drink something. Hold on. I brought some extra bottled water." Jane dug into her bag. She twisted off the cap of a Perrier and handed it over.

Becca took a sip and hoped the feeling would pass. She took another sip and then forced the rest of the bottle down. When she finished the water, she plopped her arms on the steering wheel and rested her head on top.

"Feeling any better?"

Becca didn't respond. She'd waded into a sea of trouble. Now, caught in the undertow, she didn't have the wherewithal to navigate. Paul's words echoed in her head about being careful. He hadn't thought the idea was so good to meddle in the County's work. *Leave well enough alone,* he'd told her. *You know what they say about curiosity killing the cat.*

But platitudes had never deterred her before. Tearing her granddaughter away had ripped her heart. Until she held the child in her arms again, there would be no stopping her from doing what she needed to do to mend it. With her head down on the steering wheel, Becca sobbed.

Chapter Thirty-One

"Hi, Pastor, it's Becca Wallace."

"Well, hello," Pastor Benson replied, cheerily. "How's it going? Everything okay?"

"Actually, I'm a little frazzled. I was wondering if I could come to your office. I need to share something with you."

"Today?"

"Today, if possible." She kept her tone light, hoping she wouldn't give away any signs of desperation. She hated sounding needy.

"I don't know..." he began in an undecided tone. "Let me check something here."

She squeezed her hand into a fist. *Please.* If she didn't speak with him, she'd be tempted to tell Paul what she'd done today with Jane and where they went. She feared his reaction and disapproval, and she didn't want a lecture. Facing his displeasure was something she avoided at all costs.

"I'm sorry, Becca, I thought I had more time. Looks like I have back-to-back counseling sessions this afternoon. Margie must have scheduled these."

Drat.

"Usually, she leaves more time. Anyway, I'm sorry about today, but Monday's open. How does nine o'clock sound, bright and early? That work for you?"

Becca exhaled the breath she'd been holding. "Oh, no, that's okay." She masked her irritation by feigning an upbeat air. "I understand."

"Are you positive?"

"Yes, it's okay, sir. I'll just—"

"Well, wait," he interjected. "How about...well, how about right now? I have a little time."

Her heart lightened. "Now? Oh, sure, that would be great. Can we talk on the phone instead of face-to-face?"

"Works for me."

"Great."

"Okay, what's up, my dear?"

Becca glanced at the clock. She had plenty of time before Paul came home from work. *But where to start?*

****

Later that evening

Becca lay on the sofa when the phone rang.

"Hi, Bec, it's me."

"Hey, Jane."

"Hope I'm not disturbing you."

"Of course not."

"Just checking in to make sure you're okay," she drawled.

"Sweet of you to call."

"Well?"

Becca grunted. "Been better."

"Listen, I—you know, I can't exactly relate to what you're going through not having kids myself—or grands—but I feel your pain. Really, I do. I know what heartache feels like."

Not like this. Becca cradled the phone in her ear and stared at the TV. Paul had gone to bed early, but as weary as she was, sleep, for her, wouldn't come. The only comfort she found was getting lost in an old black-and-white murder mystery where she could lean vicariously on someone else's life and give her own emotions a break.

"Did you get a chance to talk with your pastor?"

"Wait a minute." She muted the TV. "Okay, what?"

"Your pastor, did you talk to him yet?"

"Oh," she began, flatly. "Yeah, we talked." She sighed. "I told him about what we saw at the foster house, and he was shocked about Margie. Had no idea why or what to make of it."

Jane blew a breath into the phone. "Hey, crazy thought. Why don't you just call her?"

"I've thought about it. But it'll be a confrontation. I wouldn't feel comfortable."

"She's your friend, right?"

"Yeah, but..."

"At least, you'll know."

"That's just it. I'm afraid. I know it sounds silly, but I'm just too shy to say anything to her. I'm sure there's a reasonable explanation."

"Yeah, she's a two-timing friend who's complicit in taking your granddaughter."

"No, no. There has to be a reason. And what if I'm wrong? It would look...I would look so silly."

"You'll never know until you speak with her."

Becca let Jane's words settle. "You're right, I do need to talk to her," Becca said, obligingly. "But I'm just hoping Pastor will break the ice for me."

After a long silence, Jane said, "Well, I'll be praying, Bec. And Jon, too. We're here for you, honey. Let us know what else we can do to help, okay?"

"Thanks, Jane. Appreciate the prayers and everything you've done. We'll talk soon."

In the quiet of the living room, Becca mused on the situation. Seeing Margie at the foster family's house stuck like a sore that wouldn't heal. As much as Becca longed for the answers, she balked at any confrontation with Margie. Mentally, Becca played out possible ways of approaching the situation. She cringed at every scenario; in every imaginary scene, there was no way of making things seamless. All hell would break loose, and she hated the chance of losing her cool. The church already thought of her as a loser, she figured, and she didn't need any more derogatory attention. The awkward confrontation with Margie would embarrass both of them and something Becca wanted to avoid—for now.

Time dragged as though laden with molasses. Desperation set into her bones. She picked up a cigarette. Paul's lectures on the dangers of smoking along with his threats of hiding her cigarettes went nowhere. Nicotine kept her anxiety at bay. There were better ways to subdue her stress, but for now, a cigarette was the easiest. She reached for a lighter and took a long drag. She wanted to tell Paul where she had gone today but couldn't. Though keeping mum on the information only inflated her guilt. Paul believed she was sad about Tally. If he knew what was causing her additional stress, right now there would be an argument between them, and she'd be in tears again.

Becca sat in front of the mute TV and exhaled. Through the smoke, she stared blankly and tried to put all of the bad thoughts out of her head. A scripture verse came into her head, and she mentally recited the Twenty-Third Psalm over and over. She snuffed out the rest of the cigarette and went to bed.

Chapter Thirty-Two

The following morning, Becca awoke from a fitful restlessness. The discordant state of her mind precluded any more sleep, and she lay there wired. The scent of Paul's aftershave permeated the room. He probably wanted to go to church today, but she wasn't up for it. She dragged herself out of bed.

"Morning, hon," Paul said as she came into the kitchen.

"Morning."

"Made some eggs."

Becca glanced at the stove where the eggs sat. "Just toast, thanks. I can make it."

"You sure that's enough?" He watched as Becca pulled the bread from the freezer. "I left all your sections out and your vitamins," he said, nodding toward the newspaper on the table.

"Thanks." She took a slice of bread out of the bag.

Becca held onto the tradition of having the newspaper delivered, one of the ancient relics of a dying era she wanted to prop up for nostalgia's sake mainly for the word puzzles and the wedding news.

"Guess you're not going to church?" Paul glanced at the clock. "It's almost nine-thirty."

"I'm sorry, I'm just not up to it today." She put a slice of sourdough bread in the toaster. "But you can go."

"No, no. I'm not going without you," he replied and continued reading the paper.

"I know I should go, but I'm just drained."

"It's okay," he said. "We'll go next week."

Sitting at the kitchen table, the sun at her back, she nibbled a slice of buttered toast and pored through the newspaper sections:

health and wellness, lifestyle, and the others he'd left. After reading, she picked up a pencil and began the crossword puzzle. While wracking her brain for a word, something caught her eye in the ad listing —a yard sale. At the bottom of the ad copy, the address read: *665 Briarthorn Drive, Mount St. Clair.*

****

"You want to do what?" Jane exclaimed. "Again? Are you serious?"

"Never more so," Becca answered, evenly. Her stomach bubbled with excitement.

"I don't know, Bec, sounds—"

"Yes, I know." *Desperate times call for desperate measures.* Maybe it was a bad idea, but it would take a lot more to change her mind. "So, you don't think I should?"

Jane heaved a sigh. "Honey, I sure don't know what it's like to be in your shoes. My heart just aches for you. I just—I just don't know what to tell you."

"So, are you with me?"

"Yeah, of course, I'm with you. I was never not. It's that...well, you know."

"Listen, if you feel uncomfortable, I get it. I'll just go by myself. It's all right. I won't take it personally."

"What does Paul think about it?"

Becca chuckled. "Jane, now you know better than to ask that." It was the first time she laughed in a long time. It felt good. "Paul doesn't know about it. I haven't told him a thing—at least, not about this. The last time we spoke about that stupid foster house, he gave me a lecture. So, no, he's not aware of the plan." She drummed her fingers on her thigh. "He's out with a buddy from church and took the day off. They're up at Lake Nockamixon fishing."

"When were you planning on going?"

"The yard sale is today."

"I know, but when—what time?"

"I don't know. Anytime. In an hour... say, ten-thirty?"

"Okay," Jane replied.

"So, it's a plan?"

"Sure, I'll be ready."

"Great. Thanks. I'll pick you up then."

Becca hung up the phone feeling grateful for the friends in her life. Jane, her closest, was more like a sister. She understood Jane's reticence and was glad her friend didn't hold onto it. The woman led a busy life with her community volunteer work and the Visiting Angels hospice duty. There were a dozen other things her friend could be doing right now rather than planning on playing sleuth in a makeshift stakeout. The lady was a southern belle. Classy and upstanding, much like Paul. How people of Jane's and Paul's pedigrees ever found their way into her life was beyond her.

Becca, totally energized now after calling Jane, headed for the shower.

Chapter Thirty-Three

The property of 665 Briarthorn Drive morphed into an explosion of home goods that covered the front lawn from one end of the two-story colonial to the other. With all of the eye-catching attractions on display, the adjacent yard drew Becca's attention the most. The white clapboard with its black shutters did not rank among the showcase houses on the outside, but inside, it housed a precious treasure.

Her mind focused on what Tally might be doing her second weekend away from home. She'd already been signed up for T-ball, ballet, and swimming lessons at the community center. So, what could these new people offer her at the foster home that she and Paul couldn't provide? Becca didn't believe they had the child's best interests at heart. The thought pressed in like the thrust of a knife.

"I hate yard sales," Becca said to Jane. "It's like someone pleading *buy my junk*. Who'd want it?"

"I thought you liked 'em?"

"Not really."

"I thought that was the reason we came here. Or was it just because of Tally?"

Of course, it was all because of Tally. Becca lent a coy smile. "I didn't lie to you. I just asked if you were interested in going to a yard sale—in this neighborhood."

"On this street," Jane added, smartly. "You know, I've never purchased anything from a yard sale before. Though, once, I got a potato masher from my sister-in-law, Linda, who bought it for a quarter," Jane mused. "That's when I used to cook."

Becca, deep in thought, lent half an ear to Jane; bless her heart, the woman could talk, though her words faded into the background as Becca focused on her purpose for being there. All she wanted was a glimpse of Tally and the understanding she was okay in her new surroundings. *Just a glimpse, Lord.* Becca pulled the minivan to the curb and cut the engine.

"Okay, listen. I wanted to come here—not so much for the yard sale—but, as you know, to see Tally, right?"

"I know." Jane unbuckled her seat belt and lent a wry smile. "It wasn't a surprise."

"It's so important that I do, Jane." She held her hands together, prayerfully. "I've been beside myself."

"I know, honey. You don't have to convince me. The light in your pretty brown eyes hasn't been there in a while."

Becca took off her sunglasses and reached into the console for a tissue. "I have no idea whether she's even there right now—but, Lord willing, I can hope."

"I'm with you, Bec," Jane confirmed. She patted Becca's forearm.

"Okay, then." Becca wiped the lenses and put them back on. "Let's roll."

****

People milled and lingered around the tables spread with vintage dishes, glassware, kitchen items, knickknacks, costume jewelry and more glistening in the sun. In addition to the tables, there was a red bicycle, a pair of skis, exercise equipment, and several large pieces of old furniture. Becca sauntered up and assumed a place among the others as she panned her sights over the offerings with a feigned interest. She cast a curious eye here and there at the displays and circled around, attempting to blend in the best she could. One eye skimmed the sale items while the other one fixed laser-like on any movement in the adjacent yard. The real gem of a find she longed for was not here among the tables but about fifty feet away in the next yard.

The windows on the house next-door were shut and the blinds drawn. All she could discern of any life was the soft purr of the central AC unit at the side of the house where a spray of half-spent daffodils clung to life. She wondered which window was Tally's? Did the home contain the amenities of a little girl, or was it stripped bare of the feminine touches Becca strived to give her?

Normally, on a day like today, Tally would be out in the wading pool Paul filled up for her every summer. Just the word *pool* put a smile on her face. Right now, the water in Tally's pool had all but evaporated, and the plastic lining served only the duty of collecting bugs and other debris.

Becca sidled over to the driveway where a stunning dark mahogany chest of drawers sat like an outlier among all of the other things. As disinterested as she was in the yard sale, the temptation of touching the smooth claret-colored wood tugged. She pulled one of the brass handles of the top center drawer, one where someone's undergarments most likely once were kept, and peeked inside.

The tongue-and-groove construction of wood indicated it was well made and took her back to the time she had housecleaned for old-monied Mrs. Cranston, who owned similar furniture in Bryn Mawr. "It's in its fourth generation," the woman once informed her with a sense of pride. While Becca didn't have any designs on acquiring the old piece in front of her now—multiple dents, flaws, and blemishes stood out in the bright sunlight—still, it would make a nice addition for someone, especially at the cheap price tag of only seventy-five dollars.

Jane wandered up behind her. "See anything yet?"

"Nothing." She took another look around back. The postage stamp-sized yard contained a swing set in the back and a weathered picnic table with benches on a small concrete patio.

"There's no car in the driveway," Jane said. "Probably no one is home."

Becca glanced to the side of the house. "It could be in the garage."

"That's true. Hey, I'm going to check out something"—Jane pointed a finger— "I'll be just a minute."

Becca checked the time. It felt like an hour had gone by, but it was only twenty minutes. She could have stayed all day, if it meant the chance to see Tally, but she was sensitive to Jane's schedule and didn't want to make her feel obligated to hang out all day. She strolled past the rows of things she wouldn't take if someone gave them to her for free—no amount of material goods could quench the desperation in her soul—and kept her eyes glued to the backyard of the foster home, practically willing Tally—or anyone—to come out.

The sun beat down like a hot hand on her back. She lifted her long mane of hair away from her neck to air out the place where sweat started to gather and pulled it into a pony. Her cotton T-shirt matted against her back at the waistband of her cropped khakis. A cigarette would taste good right about now, and she rummaged through her purse. Only the empty, taunting pack remained. She held the container to her nose and inhaled the last traces of tobacco.

Time moved slowly. Becca gazed at the table of jewelry and wondered how much of it was costume or the real thing? Farther down the table a ruby ring sat among some others, but upon inspecting it, she noticed it wasn't 14 kt. gold. Just a cheap knock-off. She checked the time again. Ten more minutes had passed. Now, they'd been there almost a half hour. What could she do even if she did spot Tally? On top of everything, she felt the fuzziness of a tension headache coming on.

She silently cursed the people at the County's youth services office for making her grovel like this; her desperate hope clung by a thread. The County mentioned in the initial letter that she and Paul would receive visitation rights at some point in the future, but the wording was so cold and vague, it sounded like those officials had swallowed their hearts as they described the protocols going forward. *As they saw fit*. Why couldn't they leave well enough alone? There was no purpose in this at all as far as she and Paul were concerned. Maybe it was a trial sent from the Lord to show her how to be patient, someone had told her. Pastor Benson suggested the same. Becca wasn't convinced. The custody battle was more like a tactic of Satan. She and Paul were just the fall guys.

Jane stood by one of the tables stacked with glassware, chatting with another blonde-haired woman. Busy in conversation, Jane smiled as they both bonded over the merchandize. She reached for a crystal decanter and held it as though it were a dead fish. Becca raised her hand and waved for Jane's attention. Jane caught her eye and quickly set the item down and hurried over.

"Hey, what's up. See anything?"

Becca blew out a long breath and shook her head.

Jane's shoulders slumped.

"What a waste," Becca said with disgust. "Sorry to have dragged you here, Jane."

"You want to go?" Jane put a hand to her hip. "It's fine, though, if you want to stay a bit longer. I saw some decent stuff over there. Looks like it might be real crystal." She pointed to the table with the crystal decanter. "A little chipped, but..."

Becca shook her head. "No, let's get out of here."

Jane frowned. "You sure?"

Becca nodded. "I've had enough disappointment for one afternoon. Unless you want to go buy that thing you were holding." She pointed to the glassware table. "I can wait. I'll just go bring the car around."

"No, no." Jane swatted the air. "Please. I don't need a crystal decanter that badly. Let's go."

****

Back in the car and on the way out, Briarthorn Drive eventually dead-ended in a cul-de-sac several blocks down. Becca maneuvered around the tight circle and back down the street again. In the distance up ahead, something flashed red through the trees. As she focused on it, suddenly a ball flew out into the street in front of the car.

"Whoa!" Becca yelled as she jammed her foot on the brake. She beckoned the towheaded child to retrieve the rolling ball. "Go ahead," she said and then turned to Jane. "Sorry about that."

"My heart." Jane held her hand to her chest.

"You okay?"

"Fine. Good thing you weren't going fast." She unbuckled her seat belt and retrieved the loose change and other miscellaneous items that fell out of her bag.

Becca put her foot gently back on the pedal and drove cautiously under the speed limit for the next couple of blocks. As they approached the yard sale again, she slowed to a coast. The street still remained packed with cars, and people milled about, weaving in and around the tables. But there was something different about the scene. In the adjacent driveway of the foster family sat a black SUV.

"I thought I saw something red back there. Must have been the rear brake lights on that car."

"The foster family's car." Jane's voice rose. "They're home!"

"Looks like it." Becca studied the vehicle as they slowly passed. Her stomach fluttered.

"Do you want to go back?" Jane asked as they approached the intersection of Briarthorn and Heritage.

As much as she wanted to, the pain in her head directed her otherwise. "No, my head hurts." She pressed two fingers to her right temple.

"You're probably dehydrated." Jane fumbled through her bag. "I'm pretty sure I had an extra bottle in here." She felt all around the bottom and checked the outer pockets. "Oh darn it all. Nope. Sorry about that."

"Don't worry, I'll be fine. Becca pressed her foot to the pedal and turned left at the intersection. As the car pulled away from Briarthorn, she looked back and wished she didn't have to leave. Farther down the road, she said a silent prayer for Tally.

Chapter Thirty-Four

Becca drove straight home after dropping Jane off. Her head pounded to the point of near nausea, and she hoped she wouldn't get sick in the car. With any luck, it wouldn't turn into full-blown pounding migraine. She recalled her last serious episode when a migraine hit at work and she suffered through it until the end of her shift. On that cold January evening on her way home, a wave of nausea forced her to stop the car on the side of the road where she wretched as snow began to fall.

"Paul?" she called as she entered the apartment a few minutes after three. In the silence, she figured he was still out at the lake with Ben.

She headed for the bedroom, kicked off her sneakers, and exchanged her sweaty clothes for a thin cotton robe before going to the kitchen where she retrieved a frozen bag of peas. She laid it on the counter and then opened the cabinet. The aspirin bottle held only a remnant of broken pieces that together barely equaled one tablet. *Great.* Lately, with all of the stress, there were a number of things she couldn't keep track of, and now she could add forgetting to buy aspirin to the list. She worried that one day the pressure would send her over the edge.

She poured a cold glass of water from the refrigerator decanter, downed the last of the aspirin powder, and then followed it with a second glass. With the bag of peas on her head, she settled on the living room couch and rested until she fell asleep.

****

Afternoon sun blazed through the living room's west-facing window. The light cast a rectangle of light on the couch where Becca gently roused from a deep sleep. She pulled the warm bag of peas from her forehead. The tension that once held her head in a vise had eased itself out. The relief gave her a lift. She sat up with renewed energy.

The apartment held only silence. Paul still hadn't returned home, and she was glad because his time away also gave her a chance for one more thing. Otherwise, if he were home, he might talk her out of what she had in mind. She got up and put the bag of peas back in the freezer.

Her mind circled around what she had seen earlier at the foster home. Whose black SUV was in the driveway? Had Tally been out with the foster parents and was back home now? She hastened to the bedroom and put on a fresh T-shirt and shorts. She then grabbed her purse and a bottled water from the fridge and left the apartment.

Becca drove along the main street through town until she hit the secondary back road leading up to Mount St. Clair. There were two ways back to the foster home according to Mapquest. One way would be the shorter of the two. The only drawback was a narrow bend in the road that by nightfall could prove dangerous.

Initially, when performing an online search, she'd read an article about Chester County roads. At the bottom of the column were comments from people who lived in the area and were familiar with them. She learned there had been more than one fatal accident over the past couple of years. The local town council demanded the County do something to curtail drivers from going too fast, especially with the double-twisting S curve along the creek bed where cars sometimes ended up. Not only mangled but submerged as well. By day, horse crossing proved effortless along the spot where the water pooled harmlessly along the road, but by night, it was anyone's guess how high the water would be.

Anxious to get to Briarthorn Drive as quickly as she could, Becca took the safer way off Route 29 and headed down Clothier Falls Road to the old Hempstead Farm before cutting over to Route 724 and then taking a series of side roads.

The scenic route canvassed the rolling hills and pristine farmland of Chester County. Hers was the only car on the road. It was a rare moment, as the sun flickered through the stands of trees in the near distance. They stood tall, keeping watch in the likeness of tall field hands along the way. The beauty lent itself to another world, and the moment reminded her of a car commercial. All that was missing was the resonant voice in the background. She rolled down the window to let in the breeze.

Thoughts about the County and what they had put her through, all because of their hasty decision to remove Tally from her home, circled in her mind. These people were beyond cruel. Nothing they did made sense. She hoped the County had sent the visitation papers with the information on when she and Paul would be able to visit Tally. Hopefully, their letter was working its way through the post office right now for tomorrow's delivery. Though she feared it may never come. She checked the time. *Five-thirty-two.* The sun shone clear without a cloud in the sky.

As she turned onto Briarthorn Drive, the butterflies in her stomach went from a gentle flutter to all out dancing. Up ahead, a few cars lined the side of the road, but the volume waned considerably from earlier in the day. Most of the tables from the yard sale were relatively empty. The skis must have sold as they were no longer propped up against the tree, but the huge chest of drawers still stood like a behemoth. Next-door, the black SUV was still parked in the driveway.

Becca drove a few feet past the white clapboard and cut the engine. The blinds remained drawn. She hoped Tally was somewhere outside on the property—sitting on the steps or in the backyard—and craned her neck for a peek. Thoughts ran through her head as the scenarios played out: Stay inside the car and spy on the property? Leave the car and lurk? Either way, it could take a while. In her newly acquired detective role, she adopted a sudden appreciation for the patience of those who made a career out of it.

As the sun dipped lower, the backs of her thighs started to stick to the leather seat. A fuzziness filled her head. She braced for a migraine relapse and hoped the feeling would soon pass. The water bottle called. She twisted the cap off and in four big gulps devoured the contents. She leaned back and waited for the tension to ease.

Her cell buzzed. She looked down at her phone. The call was from Pastor Benson. Her phone had been set to voicemail, and she quickly checked to see if he left a message. He did. *I spoke to Margie and received some news I'd like to share with you.* As much as she wanted to hear the entire message, something else attracted her attention.

A glimpse of something moving caught her eye behind the right corner of the house. There was no mistaking it. She saw a flash of white, and through her partially open car window, she heard the voice of a little girl.

Chapter Thirty-Five

Becca's ears strained. *It must be Tally*! She was sure she had heard her granddaughter's voice but couldn't discern the little girl's mood. A happy chortle or a yelp of fear? Her heart kicked into second gear. There was nothing at this point to keep her inside the car. It was time to *do* something.

She got out as casually as possible—not too fast, not too determined—and ambled down the sidewalk. She purposefully took her time, posing, at first, like someone simply out for a leisurely walk. If only she had a dog by her side to constrain her steps from moving too fast. A sniffing pooch would be the perfect foil for lending credibility and masking her intent. In the big city, her behavior would be called mere idling or, at worst, loitering. Out in the upper-middle-class suburbia, strange lingering behavior could the draw the curiosity of nosey neighbors.

She bent down and retied her already perfectly tied shoelace and then stood up and pretended to look at something important on her phone. Moments later, she cast a nonchalant gaze down the street in an innocent manner as though waiting for a ride. Her relaxed posture contradicted the tension inside. There could have been a neon sign on top of her head reading *I don't belong here.*

As she performed her act, a car passed; seconds later, another one flew by. She waved as though lending a familiarity she didn't own. Despite the oddness of how she felt in keeping up with the fake persona—like a jigsaw puzzle piece squeezed into the wrong spot—she hoped her caper went unnoticed.

In the peace of the tranquil neighborhood, amid the chirping of hungry birds out foraging, the sound of a child's voice came again. Did it originate from the backyard of the colonial or the white clapboard? She thought she had seen a flash of white earlier. Now, she couldn't be sure from which yard the voice had come, since the two yards were relatively conjoined.

The large mahogany chest still stood on the driveway at the top of the hill. The drawers had been taken out and were sitting on the macadam. She walked up the incline and all the while kept her eyes peeled on the backyard of the foster home.

Moments later, a flash of white caught her eye again. A little girl's white top. Her heart lifted. The outfit didn't look familiar, but the child did. Tally! As delighted as she was, Becca wondered where the awful clothes the child wore had come from. The top looked old and fit way too tightly from what she could tell, and the shorts, as well, clung too snugly as though they were a toddler's hand-me-downs. Mud and grass marks stained her sneakers. Becca's heart tore. *Was Tally crying?*

With every ounce of restraint, Becca held back from rushing toward her granddaughter. Something said to wait. Not giving in to her instinct to swoop in and protect, she held back and just stared from behind the tall chest.

Tally limped by the back fence. She sat down on the grass and folded one leg up close to her body. Becca's heart tugged. Tally pressed the tail of her shirt to her knee. *Did she scrape it?*

"Tally!" A booming voice shot out from somewhere beyond.

Becca's heart lurched at the sound of the male voice. The father? The reality of the situation hit home. There was a new family in Tally's life. As awful as the truth was, the sound of the man's voice didn't diminish Becca's reserve; oddly, it inflated her place in Tally's world—at least, in her own mind. After all, this man was a total stranger. He'd never be able to break the ties that bound her to the child, her beloved Tally. She was Tally's *Mom-Mom*. Nothing could take away from *that* reality.

"Coming," Tally called back. Her voice sounded strangled, as though she was in pain. *Did she just wipe away a tear?*

It took everything Becca could harness not to leap out from behind the tall wooden chest. Then something in her snapped. This may be her last chance to see her granddaughter. She could no longer fight her reserve.

"Tally," she called in the loudest stage whisper she could. Becca hoped the child would hear before she got too far away from the fence. "Tally," she repeated.

Tally turned around, and the expression on her face melted into joy. "Mom-Mom!" she cried. In a heartbeat, she ran toward the fence. Becca came out from behind the chest and met her.

"Shhh, baby," Becca coaxed. She squatted down behind the fence face-to-face with her.

"Mom-Mom!"

She palmed Tally's mouth. "Keep your voice down, honey. We mustn't let anyone know." She took Tally's hand in hers and caressed it as best she could through the chain links, taking in the moment. "I've missed you so much, baby."

"Mom-Mom, why did they take me away?" she whimpered. "Why am I here?"

"I don't know, honey, your grandfather and I never permitted it, and we're not happy about it—not in the least." She spoke in a rough whisper. "You understand that, right?"

Tally whined, "I don't like it here, Mom-Mom. I want—"

"Shhh, honey." Becca feared the foster parents might come out and see them together and word would get back to the County.

"Mom-Mom, I want to come home." She grabbed onto Becca's hand.

"I know, baby, I know. We want you home, too."

Like butter, Becca's heart melted and Tally's wish was the knife. The child's beseeching eyes didn't need to say any more. Becca knew what she had to do and quickly scanned the backyard. With a deep breath, she reached over the fence and grabbed Tally by the waist, lifting her up and over the barbed wire. The child was heavier than she remembered. On the way down, the tail of Tally's top snagged on a frayed piece of wire sticking out at the top. *Oh, not now!* Becca yanked at the stubborn grip it held, and in her haste the shirt tore, but Tally was now safely on the other side.

"May I help you?" came a deep voice. A buff man with a scruffy beard in a T-shirt and cutoff jeans stood at the edge of the patio.

Becca gasped. Her heart hammered as though she'd been caught stealing. Her feet weighed heavy as clay as she stared into his eyes. Reality hit like a truck. The cold, hard eyes of her ex-husband, Rob "Ice" McGregor, stared back.

Chapter Thirty-Six

Becca froze. Her knees quivered as she stood aghast at what she saw. She pressed her fingers more tightly around Tally's and wished this was only another bad dream. She couldn't fathom that she was staring into the face of the man she had run away from years before.

"Becca, we meet again," her ex said with fake cordiality. He took a step toward them.

She could feel her heartbeat in her ears. "R-Rob?" she stuttered.

"Yes, Becca, it's me." He gave her a devious smile as he raised his hands up at his sides before slapping them back down against his body. "In all my glory."

The muscles of his arms were beefy as though he'd pumped iron. She shivered inwardly at his strength and remembered the days when he held her in those arms while kissing her neck. Now, scrawled in tattoos, they revolted her. His smile didn't resonate as real but grotesque. His dark hair had blonde streaks. Highlights were currently the fad of millennials. What was he trying to prove?

"We—we thought you were—"

"Dead, Becca?" he said, smartly. "Is that what you were going to say?"

"Y-yes, we thought...I mean, Uncle Billy told us—"

"Told you what? That I drank myself to death? Or maybe, the truth?"

"Truth? I...I don't know what you're talking about," she stammered.

He stepped closer and cleared his throat. The guttural sound of phlegm as he spewed it out turned her stomach. His face grew sharp as though chiseled by an angry sculptor. His eyes bored into hers.

"Here, let me tell you a little bit about the *truth*." He took another step closer. "Our *son,* our beloved Jason, tried to kill me."

Becca shook her head, trembling. "No, no, that's impossible," she shot back. "Jason wouldn't do that."

She had half a mind to tell him he was crazy but thought better of it. He might take it the wrong way, and she feared his reaction. So far, she had an equal hand, though her knees buckled uncontrollably. The glaze in his eyes spoke volumes. *Was he on something?* She didn't say any more. She waited him out and gave him the benefit of the doubt. With Tally in between them, she didn't know what he might do and didn't want to risk agitating him further.

Rob grinned devilishly and nodded his head in double time. "Yes, Becca. That's exactly what he did."

"When? What are you talking about?" The words caught in her throat and came out thin and scratchy. She hated sounding vulnerable. She needed to be bold, for Tally's sake. Inflated by her disgust, she barked, "What are you saying? Jason is a killer?" The words sent her spine tingling. The boldness of her false bravado buoyed her. Bullies loved dominance, but she'd had enough of that when they were married. No more. Now, it was her turn at playing the bully.

"That's right, Becca," he barked. Spit flew out of his mouth. "I remember the day like it was yesterday—we got into a fight. Over you. Up in the mountains. He was so protective of his precious mother. Does he know that you pulled a knife on me, Becca? Does he know how you yourself probably wanted me dead?"

Rage flew up inside her, and her face burned. "I never wanted you *dead,* Rob. I kept a knife by my side for my own self-protection." Her words came out breathy and clipped. "It was from *you* that I was protecting myself. From you!"

Becca breathed shallowly as adrenaline coursed through her body. She glanced down at Tally whose face froze in fear.

"He left me for dead!" Rob shouted. "Dead. Do you hear me?"

"I wasn't there, Rob. So I don't know anything about that day. When Jason came home from the mountains, he acted out of sorts as I vaguely recall. But I don't remember him being any more so than usual. He's always been a sensitive kid, so it could have been anything."

Rob's lips curled into a cold grin. "So, he never told you, is that it? Never told you that I'd fallen from a cliff? Left abandoned? That kid is dumber than I gave him credit for."

"Jason is not dumb," she cried. "He's a good kid—or was—but I know my boy's heart. He's not a killer." Her anger stirred, and she pictured her fist punching him in the gut. "How dare you say that."

"The boy hated me and we both know it," he growled. He peered down at Tally. "But you don't, right Tally? You like living here with me, don't you?" His voice dripped in saccharin sweetness as he crouched to meet her eye-to-eye.

Tally flinched. "No, no, I don't want to be here!" the child shouted. She squeezed Becca's hand in both of hers and murmured "Mom-Mom" under her breath. Becca squeezed back for reassurance.

"It's all right, Tally," Becca comforted. Her racing heart betrayed her words. *Lord, if you're here, please send me an angel.*

Rob moved another step closer to the fence. Together, Becca and Tally backed up. Then Becca flew into panic mode, and she covered Tally with her arms, protecting her like a mother would her cub. "Just how did you get awarded custody of her anyway, Rob?" Becca demanded. "How did you pull that one?"

"Well, you have your secrets, Becca, and I have mine." At that, he hurdled himself over the fence.

Becca startled. She immediately let go of Tally's hand and shoved her away. "Run, Tally! Run to the car!" Then she squared up and sent her foot flying up into his groin.

Rob's face gnarled as he bowled over. He let out a muffled expletive while the rage in his eyes threatened like a wild animal.

The door slammed on the minivan, signaling Tally was safe inside.

In a nanosecond, Becca geared up and tore away, knowing he'd be right on her heels. Though she didn't dare turn around to check. The reality that he was close enough to tackle her was enough incentive to keep herself moving.

She passed the tall mahogany armoire still sitting on the driveway. As if by instinct, she ran around the back of the chest, grabbed both sides, and shoved it with all the strength she could muster. The heavy wood tilted backward and caught him by surprise. The armoire landed with a thud as she raced down the driveway.

Once in the car, Becca locked the doors and quickly inserted the key into the ignition. Tally sniffled in the backseat. "Mom-Mom, I'm scared."

"It's okay, baby. We're going to be all right. God's looking out for us," she called back to her as the engine roared to life.

Becca put the car in gear and shot a glance out of the passenger side window just as Tally screamed. A hand clawed at the half-open window, and the maniacal glazed eyes of her ex-husband stared back at them.

Chapter Thirty-Seven

Becca jammed her foot on the gas pedal and tore out. She sped down the road but kept a keen eye out for any children or stray balls destined to cross her path. At every stop sign, she paused instead of making the requisite stop mandated by law. Her hands shook at the wheel. She hoped a cop wasn't around. This was an emergency.

Her mind swirled with images of what just happened. *How on God's green earth did Rob get foster care custody? Or why?* Her heart beat out of her chest, and she feared having a heart attack. *Just breathe, Becca.* Then a fresh stab of panic hit. There was no way out. Briarthorn Drive ended in a cul-de-sac. She was going in the wrong direction!

"Tally, you okay, honey?" Becca tried to keep the anxiety out of her voice.

Through the child's sniffles, Becca heard a sweet, "Yes, Mom-Mom." She melted at the sound of her granddaughter's innocent voice.

"Put your seat belt on, Tal," she instructed, eyeing her in the rearview mirror. She wanted so much to hold her and tell her everything would be fine, and she hoped what was happening wouldn't leave a permanent impression on the child. For now, making sure she was buckled in was the only reassurance she could offer.

Images of the court hearing flashed in her mind: the stern judge banging his gavel, her lawyer Tony's irksome expression and his sweating brow. She seethed inwardly at the egregiousness of the whole child custody system. Acid churned in her stomach. How dare they put her and her family though this. Because of the slip of her tongue in an off moment of misplaced judgment they thought she was *unhinged*? Or unfit to take care of the child any longer?

At the approach to the cul-de-sac, she wished that she could keep driving, the farther away from his house, the better. The thought of having to go back the other way and return to the scene of her worst nightmare caused her body to quake. As she made the turn around the circle, she bit her lip. Her heart crept up into her throat as she drove back down the street. Hopefully, he wasn't outside waiting by the curb. Surely, he knew there was no way out in the direction she'd gone. If only her minivan could slip by invisibly.

At the approach to his house, she held her breath, not wanting to look, but a keen curiosity took over. *Please don't be there... please don't be there.* Instead of turning her head, she shifted her eyes and looked askance. The SUV was gone. She exhaled the breath she'd been holding. *Thank you, Lord!*

The sun hung low in the sky now; the rays darted through the pines. Her sense of time said it was at least approaching seven o'clock, and she hoped Paul was home and wasn't worried by her absence. He must have gotten back by now. *What will he think when Tally comes through the door?*

At the next intersection, she turned at Heritage Lane and followed it down to Route 724. At the junction by the old covered bridge, she took the winding route home along the river. Normally, the scenic route relaxed her. Now, she couldn't get home fast enough. Her thoughts raced.

Over the next few miles, the trees overhanging both sides of the roadway obscured most of the light, lending the sense of an early nightfall.

A few minutes into the drive back, Becca calmed down. The patter of her heart simmered back to normal, and her breathing eased in and out without any gasping. She glanced back at Tally. "You okay, honey?"

Silence.

Becca, curious about why Tally was fidgeting in her seat, asked, "Honey, is your seat belt on?"

"Mom-Mom?"

"Yes, honey?"

"I think someone is following us."

Becca's gaze snapped to the rearview mirror. There was a vehicle behind them, but there was bound to be someone else on the same road. Though, now, a seed of doubt grew. Her pulse ticked faster. *Was it him*? Rob's SUV was gone when they had passed his house, and the thought of him actually pursuing her and Tally jarred her sensibilities all over again. Even the gorgeous scenery around her could not distract from the burgeoning fear inside.

"We'll be okay," she reassured with as much lightness in her voice as she could muster. "The road is narrow, Tal, so there's no other place the car behind us can go. Keep your seat belt on, okay?" Her light tone betrayed her heart. Something wasn't right, though she hoped it was just her overactive imagination giving her pause. *Is he following me?*

Chapter Thirty-Eight

Becca gripped the wheel tightly. Her fingers throbbed. The tense pressure in her back pressed in like a bolt of steel wedged between her shoulder blades. The narrow road snaked around overhanging rocks and wide-limbed trees, and she kept her foot pressed hard on the pedal, trying to put more distance between her minivan and the car tailing behind. With the limited visibility, she didn't dare drive too far over the speed limit. At one point, the trailing car's high beams flashed, but then she thought it may have been just the change in the road surface, which occasionally rose and dipped along the road. Or was someone flashing them on purpose?

"Mom-Mom, I'm scared."

"Nothing to be frightened about, Tal," she soothed. "God has his eye on us, remember?" Becca laced her words with a smile in her voice, wishing she could own them. *Lord, please take this wheel. Please keep us safe.*

The creek alongside the roadway meandered through the countryside, curling with frothy foam over the jutting rocks and boulders. The scene took her back to the time she had traveled the rapids while on a rafting trip in the Poconos, the idyllic day when she was falling in love with Rob. Now, the scene before her quickly dashed the pleasantries of that afternoon's infatuation and reality hit. This was no pleasure cruise. For all she knew, he was right behind her.

Becca took the twists and turns like a racecar driver pulling out of the pack. As she rounded another curve in the road, overly bright headlights splashed in her face from a vehicle heading toward her. The halogen beams blinded her for a moment, and she tapped the brakes. Without seeing a guardrail, she feared going too fast. She slowed her speed. Every few seconds, she shot her gaze at the rearview mirror, trying to gauge the driver following closely behind. In fear of holding up traffic, she pressed her foot down to get back up to speed...35, 40, 45. She looked back again. The headlights behind her were gone. *Phew.* She wished she weren't so paranoid, but she couldn't help herself. She'd read too many books and watched too many horror films. The stories were fiction, yet they captivated her and cemented themselves in her mind.

She glanced back at Tally, who stared out the window. "You doing all right, Tal?" Becca checked to see if Tally was still safely buckled in the seat belt.

"Uh huh," the child answered. Tally craned her neck around. "I don't see anyone following us now, Mom-Mom."

Becca's tension eased. They were almost home. The sun flirted at the horizon now, Becca's favorite time of day. She admired the stately, silhouetted trees of Valley Forge and wondered if they had been there at the time of George Washington's trek across the frozen landscape during the Revolutionary War. The trees towered over the roadway on both sides. The branches arched together as though making a bridge of love. How blessed to live in America, especially the area of such rich history. If it hadn't been for the situation that just happened, she'd be able to appreciate it more. Yet, there was always tomorrow. *Thank you, Lord, for taking us safely home.*

Bump. Something jolted the car from behind, sending the car rocking.

"Hey!" she yelled. Her gaze shot to the rearview mirror. A car's grill loomed. *What are you doing, you idiot?* She wanted to scream bloody expletives, but with Tally in the backseat, she bit her tongue and cursed inwardly. *What's this person doing?*

"Mom-Mom." Tally's fear returned.

"Stay cool, baby. Mom-Mom has this."

She gripped the wheel tighter to keep from shaking, although it didn't help. Her whole body coursed with adrenaline. *Breathe, Becca. Just one breath at a time. Lord, where are you?* Her heart pounded so loudly that she felt the panicky thump of her heartbeat in her ears, and she struggled to stay the course. She carefully tapped the brakes as the road curved downward along the rushing river. *Does this road ever end?* She glanced up again and caught a glimpse of the driver as some space opened up between the cars. A man was at the wheel. His mouth curved into a wicked grin. No doubt, the driver behind them was Rob.

Oh, he's insane. "So, it's gonna be like that, huh? You want to play dirty, is that it?" she yelled. "I'll play with you." Her fight-or-flight instinct kicked in, and the adrenaline surge inflated her with courage she didn't know she had.

"I'm scared," Tally screamed.

"Stay calm and remain in your seat, Tally," Becca said, firmly. "Just do as I say, honey. Everything will be fine."

Desperate for what to do next, Becca had no idea how to get him off her tail. She said a quick, panicked prayer for God's wisdom. *What to do, Lord? Please give me a sign.*

Up around the bend, a slice of low-lying sunlight pierced though a small clearing in the pines. Becca pressed her foot down and slowly inched above the speed limit. With every increase in speed, the tailing vehicle remained right behind her, gaining to close the gap. Before he could bump her again, a still, small voice said to slow down. It was not something she would have chosen to do. Instinctively, her heart told her to speed up and get as far away as possible lest he bump her off the road. Every nerve in her body tingled as she took her foot off the pedal and the vehicle slowed from 48...45...40...to 39 m.p.h.

She glanced in the rearview mirror. He was still hot on her tail. *He wants me dead.* Her heart beat out of her chest as he sped up again. Moments later, the yellow S curve sign loomed in the dimness. *I'm going too fast!* Like an out-of-control roller coaster, she was in for the duration. If she braked now, he'd slam right into her. Speed up and she'd lose control.

She glanced up at the mirror again and saw him wildly gunning down on her. *Dear Lord*. In a snap decision, right before the curve, she abruptly turned the wheel into a cutout in the road and slammed her foot on the brake pedal. The tires hit the gravel, and she pumped the brakes hard as the car swerved on the uneven ground. She held her breath as momentum swept the vehicle into a 180 before it slid precariously close to the bank of the river. *Oh, no! Please, God, no!*

In the last second, before she covered her face to brace for impact, a flash of silver zoomed by in her peripheral vision, and she heard the deadly sound of crunching metal before she looked up and saw her ex-husband's truck overturned in the river.

Chapter Thirty-Nine

The next day

Becca slowly awakened to the pleasant trilling of birds in the trees through the partially open window. She opened her eyes.

"Hi, honey. How do you feel?"

"Hi," she replied, groggily.

"Sleep well?"

"I guess. Had some weird dreams." A faint remembrance of what had happened out on the road sparked in her otherwise fuzzy mind. She pushed the images away.

"Brought you some tea." Paul laid the cup on the bedside table.

"Thanks." She tried to sit up.

He reached around and placed a second pillow behind her, and she relaxed into the softness. "There you go."

"My head hurts." She rubbed her forehead back and forth, and he frowned. "It's just a headache." She gave him a reassuring half-smile. "Not to worry."

"We'll have to keep an eye on it. Might be a concussion."

Becca waved the air. "It's just my usual thing. The doctor said—"

"The doctor..." he interjected, "said to check in to let him know how you're progressing. He wants to know all of your symptoms." Paul's brow tightened as he picked up the cup of tea and handed it to her. "It's the kind you were asking for, Lemon Verbena."

She took the cup.

"Careful, it's very hot," he warned. "I put some honey in it."

She took a sip and savored the sweetness. “Perfect, thanks. What time is it?”

“A little after four.”

“That late already?” She closed her eyes and tossed her head back. “Now, I’ve just wasted a whole day.”

“You needed your rest, hon. I didn’t have the heart to wake you.”

“Where’s Tally? Is she napping?”

“She was. She’s in the living room watching TV right now.”

“How is she?”

“She’ll be fine, the doctor said,” he confirmed with a nod. “By the way, you have a visitor.”

“A visitor—who?”

“Pastor Benson.”

Becca slipped out from under the comforter and placed her bare feet on the hardwood floor. Sore from the minor bruises caused by being jolted around in the car yesterday, she hid her discomfort as best she could. It wasn’t the worst pain she ever encountered, considering all that she’d been through.

Coming through the tragic mishap on the road with her life and Tally’s spared, she believed God truly had sent her an angel. The fact that her ex-husband was now dead as a result of his reckless driving gave her mixed emotions. Both pity and sadness draped like sackcloth. Even though she thought he was already dead all these years, the fact that he truly did die and had departed from earth impacted her deeply. That she was involved somehow in his demise made the moment all the more regretful. Bittersweet.

“You up for a visit?” Pastor Benson asked. He greeted her with a broad smile as she entered the living room. The sweet charm of her favorite pastor never failed to uplift her spirits. Like a loving father, Pastor Benson filled a place in her heart where her own dearly departed father left off.

"Hi, Pastor." She self-consciously threaded her hand through her hair, hoping she didn't look too bedraggled.

"How're you feeling there?"

She lent a half-smile. "I'll live." She placed a hand on her lower back. "Just some minor swelling and bruises."

"We're so glad you're okay, Becca. The whole church has been praying through the prayer chain." He cupped her hand in both of his. "We know you've been through a lot."

Becca nodded in appreciation.

"Sit down over here, Pastor," Paul said. He patted the headrest of his favorite chair.

Pastor sat down, and Paul and Becca took the sofa where Tally sat watching cartoons. Paul lowered the sound a bit and then lifted his granddaughter up and placed her in his lap.

The pastor smiled at the exchange and then turned his attention to Becca. "Listen, I don't want to stay long, but among other things, I just wanted to address your concerns about Margie the other day when you called me."

The incongruity of seeing Margie at the foster care home caused Becca much consternation. She shifted and braced for his reply.

"I wanted to let you know that I spoke with her, and she said there was nothing between her and your ex-husband...Rob, was it?"

Becca nodded.

"Yes, well," he continued. "Turns out she was delivering welcome baskets in the neighborhood when you saw her." His lips curled.

"But he was carrying her in his arms," Becca replied, still curious.

Pastor shook his head. "Poor girl twisted her ankle somehow and fell. Apparently, she couldn't walk back to her car."

"Oh, no. You mean I've been thinking...?" She raised her hand to her mouth.

"Well, appearances can be deceiving," the pastor said.

"Apparently," she exclaimed, her heart lifting. "Pastor, I'm so glad to know this. And all this time I thought she was...well, never mind."

"It sure looked like circumstantial evidence." He nodded. "I can see how you'd come to an awkward conclusion."

"Exactly. And at that point, I didn't know the identity of the foster father. Had no clue. The paperwork never mentioned the name, right?" She glanced at Paul. "I can't even imagine what my reaction would have been had I known it was Rob."

"It was a blessing you didn't," Pastor Benson said.

Paul put his arm around her as she leaned into his shoulder.

Pastor frowned. "Poor Margie has had her share of troubles. On top of her twisted ankle, she recently lost her only remaining relative—her great-aunt."

"Oh, so sorry to hear that," Becca replied.

"She called yesterday morning to tell me she'd be traveling over the next couple of days to West Virginia." He slapped his palms together and stood. "Well, listen, I don't want to take up any more of your time. That's basically all I wanted to share and, of course, check in on how you were."

"It's no bother, Pastor," Paul said.

"You're always welcome," she added. "Can we offer you anything...coffee, tea?"

"No, no,"—he waved his palm—"I've got to be on my way." He stood and stepped toward the door. "Oh," he said, softly, "we're delighted you're all right. It could have been a different story, you know."

Becca nodded. She and Paul walked him to the door.

"As bittersweet as it is, you're a blessed woman." He turned to her and extended his hands.

Becca's eyes teared up as he wrapped his arms around her. "Thanks, Pastor. I know. Actually, as you always say, I'm better than I deserve."

Chapter Forty

Seven months later

"I'll get it," shouted Tally as she raced for the door.

"Ask who it is first, Tal," Becca called from the kitchen.

"Who is it?" Tally asked, loudly.

Paul stood behind her and checked the peephole. Standing at the door were Tally's parents, Jason and Lark.

"Tally!" they shouted in unison as the door opened. They reached down to scoop her up in their arms together.

Their faces glowed with pure love for the child. Becca's heart filled at the exchange and soon could no longer contain it as tears drew to her eyes. She was concerned at first about Tally's reaction as her granddaughter hadn't seen them in so long. Would the bond still be there? It turned out that seeing Tally bask in the attention, there was no doubt in Becca's mind that this moment was an answer to prayer.

****

"Everybody get enough to eat?" Becca asked at the table. "I have more lamb still warm on the stove if anybody wants any... Jason?"

"I'm good," he replied. He spit the ice cube he'd been sucking back into the glass. "I already had two helpings."

"Lark?"

Becca's daughter-in-law shook her head demurely. "It was delicious, though."

"You're welcome to have more." Becca looked at Paul. "Honey?"

He shook his head and patted his stomach. “I’m good, babe.”

“Mom-Mom, I want my dessert now.”

Becca brightened. “Ah, yes, we have strawberry shortcake waiting in the wings.” She picked up a serving plate. “Okay, Tally, come help me serve it.”

****

“I can’t tell you”—Becca shot a glance at Paul—“how grateful we are to have you both back. We’re just so happy you guys are together.” She cast her gaze back and forth between her son and daughter-in-law, who both sat on the sofa, while she and Paul shared his big chair. Lark and Jason hadn’t been together in so long, she thought this day would never come.

“Folks at church have been asking about you,” Paul said.

“Both of you,” added Becca. “Are you still counseling with Pastor Benson?”

“About once a month,” Lark replied. “Mainly, Jason goes.” She put her hand on his leg. “You like him, right?”

He nodded.

Becca didn’t want to pry too much. She prayed the pastor could lend his wisdom where she and Paul had failed to break through. From what Pastor Benson shared, Jason’s spirit slowly improved in the few months they’d been meeting together. Ever since he found out he hadn’t been responsible for his father’s death, Pastor said there was a discernable change. After all of the years Jason had suffered with the burden of guilt, it may have been the reason he turned to drugs in the first place.

“Maybe I shouldn’t be saying this, honey, but Pastor Benson—while he’s kept your sessions confidential—he did mention to me that he’s seen a great change in you. For the better.”

The young man shrugged. “I guess.”

“You’ve been through a lot, Jason. There’s a lot to unload. Just remember, like everything, good things usually take time. So, I just wanted to encourage you to keep on keeping on, like Pastor always says to us." She smiled and glanced at Paul.

"So, how are you guys doing financially?" Paul questioned. "If you need a loan or anything, we can discuss it."

"Actually, we're doing okay, for now," Lark said. "Jason's working for R&H Landscaping, and I'm a temp secretary. The County helped me find something."

"That's wonderful," Becca said.

Jason cleared his throat. "But we have a favor to ask you."

Becca sat up as Lark and Jason glanced at each other.

"Well," Jason began. "We...um..." He crossed his arms over his chest.

"What, Jas?" Becca said.

"What we're trying to ask is..." Lark began. "We'd love for you to continue taking care of Tally." She paused. "Maybe not forever, but until we can get ourselves together in every way...financially and...well, we just think she's been in such a good place with you guys and everything."

Becca's heart surged with joy. "But the court ruled in your favor." She glanced at Paul. "Beginning next year, we've been instructed to give custody back. I mean, we thought that was what you wanted...to take care of your daughter yourselves."

Lark dropped her gaze sheepishly into her lap. "It was. It is. It really still is, but—but my mom was a big part of it, too. She wanted—still wants Tally and all—"

"But we think you'd do a better job, Mom," Jason interjected.

"You see, my mom's been diagnosed with colon cancer," Lark said, softly.

Paul squeezed Becca's hand, and she squeezed back. She kept her joy in check, not wanting to dance at Athena's diagnosis, for which she sympathized. But the words of her son and his wife came as a shockingly wonderful answer to prayer. The rush of gratitude at the news about Tally ballooned her heart.

Chapter Forty-One

Three months later

In the quiet of the living room while an old black-and-white western aired on TV, Becca and Paul lay leisurely sprawled on the sofa after a light dinner of Jarlsberg cheese, red grapes, water crackers, and wine. Becca relished nothing more on a Saturday night than relaxing at home, and she luxuriated in the moment as she snuggled up against Paul's chest. She'd always been a homebody, and now more than ever before, she understood why. If home is where the heart is, hers was right here with her family.

Becca didn't envy her friends, who'd packed their lives with novelty and busyness on weekends, like Jane and Jonathan. How restless they must have been leaving their home all the time. Maybe she was getting old, but she knew what she wanted. More than ever, contentment for her life right now in their little apartment together as a family was enough. Maybe, one day, they would have the funds for a condo or something that would provide equity for their retirement years, but for now, this would do just fine.

"Mom-Mom?" Tally called through the patio screen. "Miss Bea wants to take me and Jin-Lee out for ice cream. Can I go?"

Miss Bea stood on the patio with the girls. "Is okay, Miss Becca?" she asked, nodding.

"Yes, yes, it's fine," Becca replied as she hopped off the couch. "Wait, Tal, let me get you some money."

"No, no," Miss Bea said from the patio. She pressed her face close to the screen. "It's okay." She patted her handbag.

"Oh, that's too kind of you. Thank you, Miss Bea."

Becca tried focusing on the movie, but the *clop-clop* of horse's hooves soothed her, and she began to drift off. At one point, when someone drew a gun, the loud gunfire startled her awake. The sounds of men yelling and shooting evoked the memory of her ex-husband. His negative feelings weren't only for her; his bitterness had fallen on just about everyone he had come in contact with. He sabotaged them all in one way or another.

Becca and Paul eventually learned that apparently Rob had stolen his old army buddy Darnell Harding's silver lighter and sought revenge by burning down their house, using the lighter to implicate Darnell. Not knowing that Lark was his own daughter-in-law when he'd met her at the bar, Rob's vain pursuit of her had been an enormous blow to his ego. When he realized she shared a home with his ex-wife and the son who'd left him for dead long ago, it made the setting of the fire all the more ultimate payback—his final retribution. Later on, he had taken advantage of his army buddy's position with the County to gain foster care of Tally. No one knew his motive for the latter move, other than an unquenchable lust for retribution in the life of his ex-wife and his son's family. Thankfully, the mentally ill man would no longer interfere in their lives again.

Chapter Forty-Two

Early fall 2019
Chester County, PA

"Okay, let's go, Tal," Becca called. She slung her handbag over her shoulder. "It's time for church, honey."

"In a minute," Tally called from her room.

Paul checked his watch. "Are we walking today?"

Becca parted the vertical blinds at the patio window. "Why not? Sun's out. Looks perfect." She cracked open the sliding door as balmy Indian summer air slipped inside. "Yum, the air smells divine."

"I guess that answers my question." He picked up his Bible. "Tal, you just about ready?" he called down the hall.

"Coming," she replied. Tally stepped into the living room looking every bit a mini version of Becca as she emerged in a pink sundress and matching sandals. A tiny handbag dangled on a silver chain over her shoulder.

****

People milled inside the church vestibule as Becca, Paul, and Tally came in the door.

"Becca, glad to see you." Linda Romeo greeted her warmly and handed her a bulletin.

"And you, too," Becca replied. "I heard your mom had an operation. How's she doing?"

Linda broke into a reserved smile. "Doing great. Thanks for asking. The doctors expect a complete recovery."

Becca smiled. "Wonderful news!"

Becca mingled a bit, hugged and greeted everyone she hadn't seen in a while, and Paul followed behind her, shaking hands with some of the men. On the way to their usual spot, the second row from the back, she paused. Margie stood by the piano, and several others gathered around her. Intrigued, Becca laid her Bible on the pew. "Be right back."

As she approached the gathering, she heard someone say, "He's so beautiful." Standing at Margie's feet was an adorable dark-haired toddler about a year old.

Margie grinned broadly. "Becca!" she called. "Have you met my little guy?"

Her little guy? "Oh, my goodness, is this the little infant you—"

"The one I found, yes! Can you believe it?"

"Margie, I'm speechless." Becca crouched down to look eye-to-eye at the little boy. "Hi, there," Becca cooed. She wanted to gobble up his bright pink cheeks. "Hello, sweetie."

"His name is Curtis Jordan, named after my Curt."

Becca, on the verge of tears and overwhelmed with happiness for Margie, gave her a long embrace.

"This is beyond cool, Margie, I'm so happy for you. This is just too amazing."

"Tell me about it." Margie's smile spread ear-to-ear, and she reached for the child's hand. "C'mon, buddy. We have to get you to the nursery now," she soothed.

"I'll talk to you later," Becca said. She waved to the little boy until he was out of sight and got to her seat just as the worship leader approached the microphone.

Becca leaned into Paul. "Margie has a baby. Remember the one she found at the park last year? She adopted him. Is that incredible or what?"

Paul gave her the thumbs-up sign just as the congregation stood to sing the first hymn, "How Great Thou Art."

Emotionally moved by the words, Becca could never sing this song without crying. As she took in the moment and thought about how much God had blessed her in the past year, her heart fluttered in gratitude overload. Her eyes teared. Embarrassed by her emotions, she hoped her watery eyes would dry before her make-up smeared. *When Christ shall come / with shouts of acclamation / and take me home / what joy shall fill my heart! / Then I shall bow / in humble adoration / and there proclaim, / "My God, how great thou art!"*

Pastor Benson shared the latest prayer requests and upcoming church events before he signaled for the men to come forward and collect the morning offering. She turned around as Dominic and Mark came up the aisle, and something caught her eye. Becca nudged Paul with her elbow. "Look behind you," she whispered.

Paul turned around. His lips curled. "That's a surprise."

Becca, overcome with joy, could barely contain her feelings. Jason and Lark were sitting together in the back row. Her whole family was together and the moment so perfect, all she could say was, *How great thou art, Lord. Indeed, how great thou art.*

About the Author

"Mary will never be a mathematician," were the words of MARY CANTELL's third-grade teacher to her parents upon first meeting them. Taking this as a cue, the eight-year-old wannabe writer adopted the self-fulfilling prophecy and began pursuing her natural love of language. Graduating with a B.A. in English Writing, she later became a radio/TV broadcaster and sidelined as a newspaper columnist. Her day job found her reporting Philadelphia's traffic conditions inside an 8' × 8' booth. It was not so glamorous—at least, not from her vantage point. When she was laid off after nearly sixteen years in the news biz (and lost her newspaper column as well, all in the same week), it was a blessing to have the opportunity to write full-time. She is the author of the debut novel, *Her Glass Heart,* along with *Untying the Shadows* and *Beyond the Roses*. Her freelance writing has found publication in numerous magazines, newspapers, and book anthologies, including *Guideposts*. *Hope Another Way* is her fourth novel. www.marycantell.com

Printed in the United States
by Baker & Taylor Publisher Services